learning
to swim

learning to swim

cheryl klam

delacorte press

Published by Delacorte Press
an imprint of Random House Children's Books
a division of Random House, Inc.
New York

Delacorte Press and colophon are registered trademarks of
Random House, Inc.

www.randomhouse.com/teens

Educators and librarians, for a variety of teaching tools,
visit us at www.randomhouse.com/teachers

Library of Congress Cataloging-in-Publication Data
Klam, Cheryl.
Learning to swim / Cheryl Klam. —1st ed.
p. cm.
Summary: Seventeen-year-old Steffie and her single mom, Barbie, have
moved yet again after a married boyfriend of Barbie's left her, so when Steffie starts
falling for the lifeguard at the country club where she has a summer job, she
worries that she is becoming too much like her mother.
ISBN 978-0-385-73372-4 (trade pbk.) — ISBN 978-0-385-90387-5
(Gibraltar lib. bdg.)
[1. Mothers and daughters—Fiction.   2. Single-parent families—Fiction.
3. Adultery—Fiction.   4. Lifeguards—Fiction.   5. Swimming—Fiction.
6. Friendship—Fiction.   7. Maryland—Fiction.]   I. Title.
PZ7.K67677Lea 2007
[Fic]—dc22
2006004603

The text of this book is set in 12-point Goudy.

Book design by Kenny Holcomb

Printed in the United States of America

10 9 8 7 6 5 4 3 2 1

First Edition

For my mom,
with love

I would like to thank Esther Newberg,
Beverly Horowitz, and Claudia Gabel
for all their patience, insight, and expertise.

I would also like to thank Sadie and Lily for
allowing me to pull rank with the TV and the computer
(even though it wasn't really fair).

And finally, I would like to thank Brian
for just about everything.

Some mothers are alcoholics, some are druggies, and some are compulsive shoppers, gamblers, and/or liars. Mine suffers from one of those types of emotional, addictive diseases as well (although definitely not as serious as the ones I just listed). It's a relatively undocumented condition that I, Steffie Rogers, refer to as love lunacy.

In a nutshell: the victim of love lunacy goes from one bad affair to the next, hoping to find happiness, but usually finding the exact opposite. I've watched Barbie (Mom and I are so close—read: dysfunctional—that she insists I call her by her first name) suffer through so many heartbreaks, I could write a book on the subject. In order to help others (and myself) understand this annoying syndrome, I've mapped out the stages of the disease.

1) Secret smile. A weird lopsided, plastic-looking grin becomes plastered on Barbie's face, like she just found a stash of blue M&M's.

2) Forbidden phone call. A call that is so private Barbie must take it outside, away from me. Phone call is followed by a joyous mood.

3) Barbie bliss. May last as little as a couple weeks or as long as several months. Demonstrated by secretive movements, the humming of sappy love songs, and an almost manic burst of energy. During this period, Barbie will hint at positive things to come: "Maybe we should buy a place here and settle down," or "How would you feel if I remarried?"

4) Hot-potato phone. Barbie suddenly becomes neurotic about her cell phone, constantly checking for messages and jumping every time it rings. This sudden obsession indicates that all is not right in Neverland.

5) Schizoid mom. Relationship is clearly on the rocks. Barbie's moods swing from ecstatic to dismal, good to bad, white to black.

6) The map. Fed up or simply dumped, Barbie pulls out her map of Maryland, closes her eyes, and drops her finger.

7) The finger move. Wherever the finger lands—we move.

8) Remission. Barbie promises to never even look at another (ahem—married!) man again.

Numbers six, seven, and eight have happened to Barbie fourteen times. As a result, I've lived in fourteen towns—and I've only been alive for seventeen years. I do the math in my head on a regular basis. The end product is always the same, and it can be easily described with the following made-up adjective: sucktastic.

In all fairness, though, Barbie's not a total lunatic. Unlike most alcoholics and druggies and compulsive whatevers, she has a handle on the basics. She puts a roof over our heads, earns a decent living, and contributes to the betterment of our household, and with a genuinely, if not freakishly, upbeat attitude, I might add. Consistent exposure to her sunshiny disposition can really affect a regular person's state of mind. Case in point: When school ended in mid-June, Barbie used her love-lunacy-influenced, mind-powered tractor beam (when used on men, it's boob-powered) and convinced me to work at her office over the summer so I could learn "fiscal responsibility" and save up for tuition at the crummy community college I assume I'll be attending.

Only, Barbie's office isn't an office. It's the bar at the Tippecanoe Country Club, where she's a cocktail waitress who stuffs tips in her bra. And what do I do at this giant, fancy rich-people hangout on Jones Island?

I'm a maid. A polyester-uniform-wearing, plunger-toting maid.

Okay, considering that Barbie thought this idea

would also lead to some wacky brand of mother-daughter "fun," it's pretty obvious that she *is* a total lunatic. And to be honest, even though I love her, I don't want to be anything like her when I grow up. Especially when it comes to that hairy-chested testosterone-producing species that scientists and laypeople like to call men.

Right now, there's just one thing that stands in the way of my life's mission, which is to avoid love lunacy at all costs.

His name is Keith McKnight.

In fact, I can feel a secret smile forming on my face already. . . .

1

The day started off like every other Monday. I was hunched over a vacuum cleaner, tidying up the carpet of the ornately decorated club room at Tippecanoe (which was designed many years ago by the same people who built the glamorous Waldorf-Astoria hotel in New York). The manager, Mr. Warzog, handed me a plunger and informed me that the toilet in the boys' bathroom at the pool had overflowed. How typically sucktastic.

I would have to walk around the pool in my maid outfit, right past potential love lunacy candidate Keith, and every girl in my school. Yes, *every* girl in my school. Mora Cooper and her popular cheerleader crowd. Amy Fitz and her jocky soccer group. Even Rafaela Berkenstein and her punky friends with the dyed black hair who go around quoting obscure poets and talking about the meaning of life. They were all there, soaking up rays in their bikinis while I was walking around in my baby blue maid outfit and cleaning up stinky bathroom messes. This was not something I wanted to write about in my Good Times journal (which hadn't seen fresh ink since the fourth grade).

It was a hot, sticky afternoon in late July and the pool was jammed. I held on tight to my plunger as I maneuvered through the crowd. As I rounded the deep end, steering around the long line for the high dive, I saw Keith. Clad only in his red swim trunks and wearing his trademark Ray-Bans, he looked like a head lifeguard should: tan, tall, and totally *wow*. Keith had already graduated by the time I started at Brucker's High, but Jones Island was so tiny, everyone knew each other's business. And being a maid who was practically invisible to Tippecanoe's young and fabulous patrons, I was able to eavesdrop and get some good tidbits on Keith.

1) His mom died when he was twelve years old. (How could I not love someone with a dead mother? That would be unconscionable.)
2) When he went to my school, he was captain of the football team and a leader of a Boy Scout troop. (Word on the street was he had twenty-five merit badges!)
3) He was also homecoming king and thereby forced into dating the captain of the cheer-

leading squad, as per the International High School Social Code of Conduct. (But I never held that against him. All he was doing was obeying the law.)

4) He had sex with said cheerleader girlfriend. (This I kind of held against him. He should have been saving himself for me.)

5) He broke up with her during his freshman year at college after he started studying philosophy and registered with the Green Party. (This proved beyond a doubt that God exists.)

6) Last summer he hooked up with Mora Cooper, his current girlfriend. She was the most popular girl in my class and the new captain of the cheerleading squad. It was rumored they also had sex. (Subsequently, I bought a book on atheism and read it cover to cover.)

Naturally, like every other girl at the club, I couldn't take my eyes off his shaggy auburn hair, his long lanky limbs and toned muscles, his full lips, the dimple in his chin, his deep brown eyes . . .

Suddenly, some little boy barreled into me and *splash!* I was submerged in a hundred gallons of chlorinated water. Most people started laughing at first. They must have assumed I could swim (um . . . wrong!) and thought it was funny to see a maid get tossed into the pool. But eventually they would realize that this was more of a 911 situation than an amateur attempt at slapstick comedy. Or at least, one person would.

As soon as I stopped splashing, everything seemed to happen in slow motion. I kept my eyes open and just stared up out of the water at all those blurry faces. My plunger filled with liquid and it became an anchor, dragging me down to the bottom. Instead of letting go, I held on for dear life. I had this weird thought that I should just stay down there in the deep end until the pool closed and everyone left. Hey, it was a traumatic experience, and therefore I was entitled to a little irrational thinking.

Before I knew it, Keith had jumped in and yanked the plunger out of my hand. He wrapped his arm around me and pulled me up to the surface. All the other lifeguards helped hoist me out, and then Keith began pushing down on my stomach with his hands.

For one brief moment, I thought, *Oh my God! Keith McKnight is feeling me up!* And then I got sick.

"Back up, everyone!" Keith yelled, as if anyone wanted to get close to the spewing vomit. And then he wrapped a towel around my shoulders and led me into the lifeguard office, a small room between the bathrooms I was supposed to tend to in the first place. He sat me down on a chair and leaned over me.

"Are you okay?" he asked.

I nodded, trying to avoid looking at him.

"Are you sure?"

I nodded again.

"What happened?" he asked. "Did you have a seizure or something?"

A seizure? *I wish.* "I can't swim," I said simply, even though the story behind this was anything but simple.

"Do you want to call anyone?"

"Not my mom," I said quickly. Barbie was not known for being a pillar of strength when the chips were down. I could only imagine how she would handle the news of my near-death experience.

"How about a friend?" he asked helpfully.

I immediately thought of Alice, who is the closest thing to a best friend I've had in years. Because of the dreaded love lunacy and the equally dreaded finger moves, I never had enough time to build any good, solid, long-lasting friendships. But when I met Alice, it felt as though I'd known her forever. Maybe it was because she was a fellow maid who knew what a drag it was to clean up after people. Maybe it was because she was sweet and treated me like an adult instead of a child. Or maybe it was because she had the eyes of a wise sixty-year-old woman who had seen the world and truly experienced life. She had the body of a sixty-year-old woman too, because she was, well, sixty years old, give or take.

Just as I was about to tell him to call Alice, the door flew open and the room filled with the smell of hair spray and L'Air du Temps. There stood my mother, breathing like she was going to have a heart attack, tears the size of golf balls rolling down her cheeks. She was wearing her cocktail waitress outfit, which consisted of a short black skirt and a tight white button-down shirt with a black bow tie. Her long blond hair was curled and expertly tousled, and despite the tears, her makeup was still impeccable.

"OHMYGODohmygodohmygod!" Barbie said, practically shrieking.

I held up a hand to ward her off. "I'm all right," I said, marveling at how quickly my mom had appeared on the scene. Barbie had always *loved* drama.

My mother grabbed me and pressed my face into her humongo boobs. (They were a gift from boyfriend number seven. Before that, she hadn't been much bigger than me, a fact that I did not find encouraging.)

"You could've died." She twisted around and gave Keith an angry look, as if it was his fault that (a) I had been accidentally bumped into the pool and (b) she hadn't been there to capitalize on the significant audience when it happened. But then she turned back to me, and suddenly her eyes were welling up with more tears. She was really, truly upset by this, and given her many neuroses, I could understand why. Still, I had to make an exit—and quick—before she broke out the ugly cry.

I stood up. "I better get back to work," I mumbled, heading toward the door. Believe it or not, although my undies were still soaking wet, my outfit was almost dry. Viva la polyester.

"We're going to get you home," Barbie said, composing herself. "You're going to take the rest of the day off. Put on some comfy clothes, curl up on the couch, and watch TV." Barbie turned back toward Keith. She shrugged and said, "She just loves *America's Funniest Home Videos*. Whenever she's upset or depressed, she watches that show. She just loves it when guys get hit in the crotch."

At which point I picked up my pace, anxious to get away from Keith before Barbie could say the word "crotch" again or reveal any more of my secrets, like how old I was when I got my period. Needless to say, my mom definitely had boundary issues, and countless other issues, at that.

Thankfully, Alice had only one issue so far. She wasn't there to rescue me from all the humiliation.

Later that night, while my mom was back at work, I decided to do just what she'd suggested—curl up on the couch in my sweats and watch TV. There were times when I wished I could be like those girls who found solace in a beloved copy of a classic book, but the truth of the matter was that I liked my TV, especially videos of people falling at weddings and cats with their heads stuck in pails. In my defense, it wasn't like Jones Island was a mecca for culture. The island was a craggy piece d about three miles long and two miles wide. besides the country club, two overpriced convenience stores, a gas station, a coffee shop, and a lousy restaurant, there really wasn't much to do. In any case, I was in the middle of watching a kid get hit in the head with a softball when the doorbell rang. I straightened my sweats, ran my fingers through my hair, and answered it.

Gulp.

Keith McKnight was standing in front of me. *Keith McKnight!*

"Hi," he said, flashing me his famous grin.

"Hi," I croaked. Thankfully, I had had the common sense to turn off the TV before I answered the door.

"Alice told me where you lived. I just wanted to stop by to see how you were feeling. I hope you don't mind."

"Of course not," I said. "I'm fine, thanks." I immediately reinstated Alice to flawless status.

A lock of thick brown hair fell over his eye and he swiped it back. He was wearing a black T-shirt that showed off his muscular arms, and an old, faded pair of jeans. He was the definition of picturesque.

"Can I come in?" he asked.

"Sure," I said, glancing around nervously. Suddenly I became very aware of my surroundings. Before the bridge was built attaching Jones Island to the rest of the Eastern shore, it was just a bunch of run-down dumpy cottages built by the fishermen who lived there. Although most of the original cottages had since been torn down and replaced with perfectly landscaped McMansions, a few holdouts remained. Alice lived in one of them, and Barbie and I rented a second-floor furnished apartment in another. (Barbie was no Suze Orman, hence she'd hatched the brilliant "Let's work at the country club together" plan.)

Keith walked into the living/dining/TV room and I caught a glimpse of the Lexus he had parked outside our building. I didn't need this piece of evidence to remind me that Keith was, like, seventh-generation dripping-in-diamonds kind of wealthy. Everyone at Tippecanoe gossiped about how much life insurance money he and his dad got when his mother died. And now Keith was staring at our nasty ghetto-fied sofa, probably wondering if it was safe to park his rear end on it.

"Would you like to sit down?" I asked.

"No thanks," he said. "I can't stay." He hesitated a beat and then said, "I just wanted to ask if you would like to learn how to swim."

Everything stopped. It was so quiet I could hear my heart thumping against my chest.

"As a former Boy Scout, I'm qualified to teach you." He deepened his voice as if to counter the squeaky-clean Boy Scout image. "There'd be no charge or anything."

This had to be a dream. There was no way Keith McKnight, the hottest guy in a million-mile radius, would be standing in my living/dining/TV room offering to teach me to swim. Alice was never going to believe this one.

"So," he said, with a hint of a smile. "What do you think?"

Think? I think YES! Yes, I would love you to teach me how to swim. I would love to spend time with you, I would love to do anything at all with you!

I envisioned us in the moonlight, standing in waist-deep water. My hair would be perfectly slicked back, and I would suddenly have breasts and a really great BCBG bikini. His strong arms would be wrapped around me, holding me so close our chests would be pressed together. I would stare into his eyes and he would lean down toward me, pressing his lips against mine.

But I did not say or insinuate any of the above. Instead I said: "No thanks."

No thanks?

Say what?

How could I have said 'no thanks'? Oh yeah, Barbie. It always came back to Barbie. . . .

He nodded, walked back toward the door, and stopped. "It's not safe," he said. "You live on an island, you work by a pool. You should at least know how to stay afloat." Then he turned back toward me and said, "What are you afraid of?"

Well, if that wasn't the most loaded question of the century. Love lunacy runs in my family. I had lusted after him for the last forty-two days, knowing full well he had a girlfriend and was therefore off-limits. I was already tempted to give in to the symptoms of Barbie's full-blown condition, and that was when he and I had barely had any contact at all. Even if I could explain everything to him, he still wouldn't understand what we'd be up against.

I stood still for a moment, trying to say something, anything, but nothing came out.

"Think about it," he said softly. And then he left, politely shutting the door behind him.

2

The next day, Alice and I gabbed away about Keith's swimming lessons offer as we scrubbed the floors in the Tippecanoe dining room. Even though we'd only met six weeks ago, I was very comfortable about telling her everything. When we talked, the time went a lot faster, and to be honest, I just liked how she carried herself. She was confident and funny. I looked at her and saw what I'd be like fifty years from now.

In fact, Alice had this spirit that was just so alive and energetic, sometimes she didn't seem any older than the rest of us. I oftentimes forgot that she had visible wrinkles, wore Poise pads, and took five calcium supplements with every meal. She was that good at being young.

"So let me get this straight," Alice said as she kneeled down on the hardwood and dipped her scrub brush into a pail of soapy water. "Your mom won't let you learn how to swim because *she's* afraid of the water? That doesn't make any sense."

Alice was the oldest member of the cleaning staff, but not the weakest. She was barely five feet tall, and very slender, which made her appear fragile. Still, that didn't mean she wouldn't get down on all fours and scrub until her arms fell off. Not that she didn't have pride. Actually, Alice dyed her hair ink black every week to cover the gray, and man, did she look glamorous, as much as an aging maid could, of course.

I stopped staring at her and wiped off an area of the floor with a dry mop. "Welcome to my world."

"Well, why is she afraid? Did she almost drown or something?" she asked.

"She didn't almost drown," I replied. "My grandparents actually *did*."

Alice placed a wet hand on her chest and sighed. "Oh my. That's terrible."

Truer words couldn't have been spoken. I heard the full story only once when I was about six, and after that it had been referred to as TCI (the Catamaran Incident). Apparently, when Barbie was fourteen, her parents had gone on this second honeymoon to Costa Rica. They booked this private catamaran, and somehow her mom fell into the ocean, her dad jumped in to save her, and they both drowned. (Yes, I had considered the similarities between that event and my close call with Keith, but seriously, Tippecanoe was anything but a second honeymoon.) Then Barbie was shipped off to live with her aunt Rita for a few years and developed this water phobia before going away to college and meeting my dad, who would eventually die on her, six months before my birth.

Obviously my mother had endured a lot, and it probably was one of the reasons she had developed love lunacy and her obsession with unavailable men in the first place. But regardless, her rationale for keeping me landlocked somehow didn't seem fair.

"Just the mere suggestion of me being submerged in water for any educational or recreational purpose really freaks her out," I explained. "I'm surprised she held it somewhat together yesterday."

"Now, Steffie, mothers worry. It's part of the job description, just like wiping crap off the floor is in ours."

Hearing Alice say "crap" in her trademark grandma voice made me laugh out loud. "I know, I know. But still, this phobia of hers is a real pain."

Alice stood up and took a bottle of Murphy Oil Soap from our cleaning cart. "I'm sure it is, considering how it's getting in the way of you and Keith."

"Me?" I asked nervously. "And Keith McKnight?"

"No, Keith Richards," she said sharply.

"Who?"

Alice groaned in frustration. "Look, it's all right to like him even though he is Mora's boyfriend. And it's all right to spend time with him too. It's not like they're married."

"Whatever. He doesn't even like me like that," I said, matter-of-factly. "He probably just wants another merit badge or something."

"Regardless, the fact is that you have a crush on him and he offered you swimming lessons. Why are you transferring your feelings about your mom onto him?"

Since when had Alice become Dr. Phil? "Where are you going with this?" I asked, annoyed.

"You should accept the lessons."

I squeezed out my damp mop into the bucket and frowned.

"You're going to have to learn to swim sooner or later," Alice continued. "You might as well learn from someone you really like."

"Explain that to Barbie."

"Maybe if you told her that it was purely a matter of safety," Alice suggested.

Safety. Once again, I envisioned Keith and me in the water. He would touch his hand to my cheek and I would stand on my tiptoes, so I could look into his eyes. He would lean forward and kiss me softly. . . .

Mora Schmora. Alice was right. This was a matter of safety, for God's sake. "But I already told him no."

"So tell him you changed your mind. But make sure it's okay with your mom first. Remember, she was your age once too. She'll understand how much this means to you."

Alice was right. I had to run this by Barbie. She and I had been getting along fairly well lately, and I knew she had been doing her best to recover from love lunacy. Actually, she had been love free for almost a year now, so she deserved the chance to talk with me, see the light, and hug it out, right?

I knew this wouldn't be an easy task. Barbie's reasons for not wanting me to swim were borderline justifiable, and whenever she invoked the name of her dead parents, she was hard to dispute. Still, I had little choice. I had to give it a shot. I had to hope against hope that somewhere deeply imbedded in Barbie's mind was a sliver of rationality. I had to believe that this sliver was capable of overhauling all the neurons in her brain, and getting her to realize that passing up an opportunity to take swimming lessons (at no charge) with a lifeguard who just happened to be a hottie and quite possibly the future father of my children would be, as Alice had said so eloquently, "a real bite in the ass."

Later that evening, Barbie strolled into our kitchen, humming an unrecognizable tune. She was wearing short cutoffs and a halter top—clothes that any girl in the popular Mora Cooper crowd would've been happy to wear. The sad thing was, the clothes probably wouldn't have looked as good on them as they did on my mom.

"That smells delicious," Barbie said.

I finished stirring some Cheesy Nacho Hamburger Helper and said, "It's almost ready."

This was Barbie's favorite dish. Alice had advised me just before our shift ended that the way to get someone to do something was to do something so nice for them that they'd feel too guilty to say no. Making Cheesy Nacho Hamburger Helper was the best I could do.

As my mother sat down at the living/dining/TV room table, I took a deep breath. I had to be very careful about this. I had come to the discussion with irrefutable facts, like:

1) Learning to swim could prevent me from drowning, like I almost did yesterd■■■■■■■safety issue.
2) People drink water. Men■■■■omen are made up of 60 percent water. Therefore water and boys are good.
3) The lessons are free.
4) Since she doesn't know how to swim, I should learn how just in case she ever falls into the water. I could save her.
5) Keith is the hottest guy I know and I've been totally in love with him for forty-three days. Therefore, it would be inhumane and cruel to rob me of this opportunity. (This was only to be uttered as a last resort.)

I brought Barbie over a hot plate filled to the edges with Cheesy Nacho Hamburger Helper. She licked her lips in anticipation. Alice was right. Barbie's love of the Helper would surely take over, and she'd be putty in my hands!

The only thing I had to do was ask her in a non-confrontational way. Just kind of breezy, like "Gee, the head lifeguard at the club offered me free swim lessons, what do you think?" And then lean forward and open my eyes really wide, like I was hanging on her every word. Like I really cared about what she thought.

I sat down at the table and then swirled the Hamburger Helper around my plate with my fork for a couple of minutes.

Barbie said, "Are you all right? You seem . . . quiet."

So far so good. Perfect lead-in. I'm quiet because I'm *pensive*. Because I want *her* opinion.

I looked into Barbie's heavily blue-mascaraed eyes. *Nice and breezy*, I reminded myself. Not confrontational.

"I'm going to take swimming lessons," I announced. Oops.

My mother put down her fork and swallowed hard. She leaned forward slightly and said, "Excuse me?"

"Keith McKnight offered to teach me. He said it wasn't safe . . ."

"Who's Keith McKnight?"

"The lifeguard at the pool. The *head* lifeguard." I said

this almost proudly, as if I already had bragging rights to him.

"The one who almost let you drown yesterday?"

This was so my mother. She could turn anything around. It really was a gift.

"He didn't almost let me drown," I said. "He saved me."

She picked her fork back up and scooped up some hamburger. "Can you learn how to swim without getting in the water?"

This was the most insane thing I had ever heard. "Um . . . I don't think so."

"Then forget it," she said, before popping the bite into her mouth.

It was time to bring out the big guns. "*Everyone* thinks it's ridiculous that I don't know how to swim."

"Everyone?"

"Well, Alice does," I said, meeting Barbie's eyes.

This was not a good idea at all. My mom had this thing about Alice. Quite simply, Alice, through no fault of her own, annoyed Barbie. It was hard to believe that anyone could actually be annoyed by Alice, because Alice was, quite frankly, the nicest person I'd ever met. She was always making cookies for people and helping out sick friends and stuff. She may not have had much in terms of material things, and may have had a filthy mouth sometimes, but if I was at her house and said I wanted a blanket, she would have given me one, even if it was the only blanket she had in the world. My mother, on the other hand, wouldn't even let me borrow her precious pair of dark indigo Levi's.

"Unfortunately for you," Barbie said, "Alice is not your mother. I am. And I said no."

I should've never brought up Alice. I should've known that my mother would take it as a dare, like "I dare you to be as nice and understanding as Alice." Barbie hated dares. She always said that as far as she was concerned, dares were just thinly veiled threats. Although I wasn't exactly sure what she meant by that analogy.

All of a sudden, I felt this pain in my throat, like a welling of anxiety. Now I wanted those swim lessons more than I'd wanted anything in my life. I could not bear the thought of *not* taking those lessons. Comebacks circled through my head, like "You're everything I don't want to be!" (Used before.) Or a simple "You're right, that *is* unfortunate!" (i.e., I wish you weren't my mom). Or the immature "I don't care what you think, I'm going to do it anyway!" But I never had a chance to say any of the above-mentioned retorts because we were being serenaded by Beethoven's "Für Elise."

"Your phone is ringing," I said.

Barbie looked irritated, as if I had conjured up this

interruption in an effort to throw her off course. She grabbed her phone out of her purse and checked the number. I could tell it was a number she didn't recognize because she gave a little shrug before answering it. "Hello?"

And suddenly her whole face changed. It went from hard and kind of mean-looking to soft and flirty. "Heeeeey. How are you?" she said into the phone. And then she let out this sexy squeal of delight.

"I'll be right back," she mouthed to me, flashing me a little smile, as if instead of being on the edge of a gigantic war, we had been talking about the weather.

Left alone in the kitchen with a lukewarm dish of Cheesy Nacho Hamburger Helper, I felt a pit form in the base of my stomach.

Stage two: the forbidden phone call.

And just like that, everything changed.

Suddenly, I was reliving our swimming argument fondly, as if it was at least a remnant of normality. A mother-daughter squabble not unlike the other mother-daughter squabbles occurring over plates of Cheesy Nacho Hamburger Helper across the country. If I was correct (and I was ninety-nine percent sure I was) and this was a forbidden phone call, the lack of swimming lessons was going to be the least of my problems. But there was nothing I could do except fasten my seat belt and hunker down for Ludwig's wild ride.

"Who was that?" I asked as my mother walked back into the room with a big plastic smile plastered on her face.

"Oh, that was Mr. Warzog," she said, avoiding my eyes. "I'm sorry, sweet cheeks, but it looks like I need to go in to work tonight."

I found her statement offensive on several different fronts. For one, she never called me sweet cheeks. For two, she was assuming that I was so naïve I might actually believe that she would get all excited and turn beet red just because the man I affectionately referred to as Warthog (who bore a remarkable resemblance to the Pillsbury Doughboy) had called her. For three, we were supposed to drink a liter of Diet Dr Pepper and play a rousing game of Balderdash that night (note the irony of board-game choice).

"Why?" I asked.

"I don't know why," she said, still not looking at me. She stood up and grabbed her plate. "Someone probably called in sick."

"Who?"

"I don't know," she said. And then she looked at me. "I'm sorry," she said, softening a bit. "Look, about the swimming lessons. Let's talk about it later, okay?"

She was obviously desperate to pacify me in an attempt to avoid an altercation. Normally she never would have backed away from an argument, or even entertained the possibility of reversing a decision on one of her core idiosyncrasies, like something relating to bodies of water.

"If you want," she said cheerfully, "I can drop you off at Alice's."

Considering how much Barbie disliked my hanging out with Alice, I was now one hundred percent certain my mom was about to relapse into love lunacy. And so I took a deep breath, looked her directly in the eyes, and said, "Thanks."

3

According to Alice, there was one thing in the world that was a tonic for all that ailed it: lists. It was something a girl in middle school would believe, but again, that's what made her so fun. On her refrigerator were a list of groceries she needed to get, a list of movies she wanted to see, a list of books she had to read, and a list of the hottest male actors of all time (for the record, Alice was obsessed with Keanu Reeves). She was so certain of the benefits of making lists that when I arrived at her house so angry at my mother that I was practically spewing lava, the first thing Alice did was yank out her notebook and pen. The second thing she did was fill the baby pool up with her garden hose.

I plopped down in the white plastic lawn chair and stuck my feet in the water to cool down as Alice wrote:

1) Proof that Barbie is on an illicit date.
2) Proof that Barbie is not on an illicit date.

A half hour later we were still sitting in Alice's back-yard. We had a laundry list of reasons as to why I was so certain that Barbie was about to ruin my life, and absolutely no reasons as to why this whole thing might just be a not-so-silly misunderstanding.

"Oh!" Alice said excitedly. "I have one."

2) Proof that Barbie is not on an illicit date:
She was wearing her uniform.

"That doesn't prove anything," I said. "I'm sure that after she dropped me off, she just went home and changed."

"But why would she say she was going to work? Wouldn't she come up with a better excuse? After all, she knows you can easily check."

"That's the beauty of it," I said. "She thinks because it's so easy for me to check, I won't."

"It seems so . . ."

"Crazy? Awful? Rude? Obnoxious . . . ?"

"Terrible."

I sighed a long, deep "my life is over" sigh as I picked up a pair of binoculars and focused them on the humon-gous white Mediterranean-style house across the creek, which just happened to be the residence of Keith

McKnight. I had first spotted him trimming some trees in his yard about forty-three days ago, and every time I went to Alice's place (which looked more like a sorority house than an old lady's house—there was brightly colored IKEA everywhere), I peered through the magical magnifying lenses and prayed that he'd come outside with his shirt off. Sure, I saw him topless almost every day, but that was under professional circumstances, not on his own turf.

But even the thought of a potential Keith sighting couldn't pull me out of my funk. In fact, the thought of him just made me feel worse. "I obviously can't take those swim lessons now," I announced, setting down the binoculars.

"But I thought she said you'd discuss it later."

"It doesn't matter what she says now. I need to have my wits about me. I can't afford to get love lunacy myself."

"That's ridiculous, Steffie. Swimming lessons are not going to tempt you to play park the pastrami with a married man."

Park the *what*? "Keith may not be married," I said, "but he's got a girlfriend."

"Even if he was married, it wouldn't matter. You're not your mother. I mean, look at me. Roland was a drinker. That didn't make me one."

Alice had lost her husband, Roland, to a heart attack five years before. She liked to say that they were happily married for forty years, but the truth of the matter was that they were actually married for forty-five. The reason why she didn't count the first five is because they were so bad. That would be due to the fact that, unbeknownst to Alice at the time, she had married a total drunk.

One of her all-time favorite stories was how she got Roland to stop drinking, thereby saving his life. No offense to Alice, but it hadn't sounded all that difficult. She simply gave him the old heave-ho, and he dried out in exactly two weeks, which was when he came crawling back, begging for forgiveness. I couldn't exactly throw my mother out either, although I considered going down to county court and filling out emancipation papers after every time we finger moved.

"But Roland wasn't a blood relative," I said. "Love lunacy is genetic."

Alice rolled her eyes. "Well, my father was a drinker and I didn't become one."

I could attest to that. The only alcohol Alice had in the house was a grody bottle of peppermint schnapps that was coated in about two inches of dust. "But you did marry one," I said, thinking out loud. "It's not like you totally escaped."

Alice got up and smoothed down the back of her pink clam diggers. "Stef, I know it's hard, but even if you're right about the phone call and your mother *is* on the verge of love lunacy—"

"Not on the verge. I missed the verge. I also missed

stage one and barely caught stage two. She's already on stage three."

"My point is that Barbie has done this . . . how many times before?"

"Fourteen."

"Exactly. There's not much you can do about it right now. Your mom needs to *want* to change her behavior, you can't make her."

She was right about that. God knew I had tried to make her before. I had done everything I could think of: reasoning with her calmly until I was blue in the face, yelling and screaming irrationally until I thought I was going to have a stroke, and once I even called her boyfriend and threatened to tell his wife. None of it worked. Barbie was pretty much a lost cause. That was the scariest thing about it.

"I really wish there was more I could do," Alice said. "But you can always come over here, any time you need to. *Mi casa es su casa*, and whatever."

I flashed a brave smile as I stood up and slipped my flip-flops back on. "Thanks."

She put her hands on my shoulders gently. "So do me a favor and stop beating yourself up about Barbie, okay?"

The only thing I could do was muster up a shrug.

For some reason, Alice seemed to think she had succeeded in getting me to see the light, because she shot me a very self-satisfied, pleased smile. "Do you want me to drive you home?" she asked.

"No thanks," I said. And then I dropped the bomb that wiped the smile right off her face. "I'm going to the club to see if my mom really had to work."

With that, Alice rolled her eyes and shook her head. She should've known me better than to think I'd throw in the towel so easily. For one, I was a little thick-headed, and for two, well, how could I have lived with myself if I hadn't at least tried to jump in and save my mother? If my grandfather hadn't gone in after my grandmother, he probably would have still been alive, but he would have had to spend the rest of his life knowing that he had just let his wife go.

I took a deep breath as I approached Tippecanoe. Even though the parking lot was crowded, I was able to do a quick scan and surmise that Barbie's car wasn't there. The adrenaline surged through my veins and my heart stopped pounding as my indignation grew. I'd begun to march through the parking lot when *Snap!* the toe thingy popped out of my flip-flop.

Unfortunately, these were no ordinary flip-flops. They were my pride and joy: gold gem-studded Michael Kors sandals; shoes that I had saved for a gazillion months to buy. But even a tragedy as significant as a broken shoe (one that was only a month old, thank you very much) could not deter me from my mission. So, like a true soldier, I tucked my flip-flop under my arm, walked around the enormous stone fountain with the water-spouting statue of Adonis, and stalked through Tippecanoe's heavy oak doors.

It was Tuesday night and the place was unusually packed. As I stood in the entranceway wearing my Save the Bay T-shirt, oversize green shorts (I like my clothes big and comfortable), and only one flip-flop, I was suddenly aware of how much I didn't belong there. Without my polyester suit of invisibility, my true identity was exposed. I made my way through the bevy of polo-shirted men and pearl-clad sundress-wearing women and into the bar, where I found Warthog chatting up a waitress. He didn't look happy to see me, and I had a sneaking suspicion I knew why. For one, I had the feeling that he didn't like us maids hanging around the clubhouse unless we were on the clock and in uniform. For two, no one was allowed in without shoes.

"Is my mom here?" I asked.

"She's not on the schedule tonight," he said.

"Didn't you call her in to work?"

He shook his head.

"No one is sick?"

"Nope," he said.

He was wrong about no one being sick. Because I was suddenly pretty certain that I was going to woof on club property for the second time in less than forty-eight hours. I spun around on my one good heel and made a beeline toward the bathroom, running smack into an innocent bystander off-duty lifeguard of my dreams, Keith McKnight.

"Whoa!" he said, catching me and holding me up. He was obviously dressed for dinner, as was apparent by his bright green polo shirt. Mr. McKnight was a highly respected member of Tippecanoe, and therefore Keith usually had evening meals there with the rest of the Jones Island upper crust. I had learned this thirty-eight days before, when I was wiping up a vodka-tonic spill caused by some vapid gossiping socialites who included Mora Cooper's mother.

"Sorry," I mumbled.

"Are you okay?" he asked.

My nausea miraculously evaporated when I looked into his dark brown eyes. "I'm fine. I just broke my shoe. The thingy popped out and I can't get it back in."

"Let's see," he said, plucking the shoe out of my grasp with his large hands.

Perhaps he was going for another merit badge.

As I watched him attempt to fix my flip-flop and he bit on his lower lip (so hot!), I racked my brain trying to think of something to say. And then it came to me.

"Keith, I'd really like to learn how to swim."

"Great," he said, snapping the strap back into place. "All better." Then he gave me a soft, warm, chin-dimple-expanding smile that made me forget all about the reason why I was there.

I slipped the shoe back on. "Thanks."

"Keith?" said a shrill voice behind me.

I turned around and found myself staring down Mora Cooper. Honestly, Mora and I couldn't have looked less alike. She was somehow skinny and curvy at the same time, and she had this flawless skin that practically made its own moisturizer. She also had these fabulous hazel eyes and this cute blond bob that flipped up at the ends. I, on the other hand, was a pear girl: much smaller on top than I was on the bottom. I liked that my hair was long, but it was this very one-dimensional color that could be best described as medium brown blah. My eyes? Nothing special. Just blue. My eyelashes? They were quite full, but hey, who was going to notice them when one could stare into the angelic plasticness that was Mora's face?

"Our table is ready," she said, flashing him an enchanting, yet slightly crooked, smile.

"Mora," he said. "You know Steffie, right?"

"Um . . . no," she said, as if she'd just noticed I was standing there.

Mora was not entirely correct. She might not have *known me*-known me, but she should've at least recognized me. We'd been in the same chemistry class and had even been assigned as partners until Mora had made it clear that she would rather bath in a vat of acid than use a Bunsen burner with me.

"Oh . . . wait." Mora's hazel eyes widened with recognition. "Of course. You're the maid who almost drowned yesterday. I didn't recognize you without your uniform and your . . . whatever it was you were holding on to."

"A plunger," I said.

She wrinkled her nose as if the mere memory was unpleasant. "Speaking of which," she said, "you might want to check out the ladies' room. There's a bit of a mess in the first stall."

"Mora," Keith said, reprimanding her. "Who are you? The manager?"

She smirked and then shrugged. "It *is* her job, isn't it?"

He shook his head as if annoyed. Interesting. Keith turned back toward me and right in front of Mora he said, "All right, Stef. Stop by and see me tomorrow. We'll set up a time."

Mora's smirk turned into dismay as she looked quizzically at her boyfriend. She hooked her arm in his and led him away. "What was that about?" I heard her say to him.

In an instant, my whole mood changed. Even though I hadn't found my mother and my flip-flop broke again as soon as I stepped outside, I felt as though I was drowning in bliss.

4

On Wednesday morning I almost keeled over from shock when I went into the kitchen and found Barbie (who's usually never awake before noon) sitting at the table, humming quietly as she sipped her coffee and read the paper.

"Good morning," she said cheerfully.

"Morning," I muttered as the glow from my Keith interaction evaporated. I opened the cupboard and pulled out the box of chocolate Pop-Tarts. "You're up early."

"Couldn't sleep," she said with a shrug. "Plus, it's such a beautiful day. I thought I might go for a run this morning. Get some exercise."

On Jones Island, there were always women jogging around in their bras and spandex. Barbie wasn't one of them. In fact, Barbie and I liked to joke that our idea of exercise was opening the refrigerator. In other words, if I'd needed more proof that my mother was in the throes of love lunacy, this would've been it. "How was work last night?" I asked.

She glanced at me. I could tell from the panicked look in her eyes that she knew I was on to her. So she said, "Actually, I didn't go to work."

I felt a surge of relief, as if my mom was going to come clean. How naïve of me.

"They didn't need me after all," she continued. "I would've come home, but I knew I had already screwed up our board-game night. Since you were at Alice's, I decided to call a friend and see if she wanted to meet for a drink."

Once again, I found myself wanting to believe her. I really did. But my mom didn't have any friends. The closest thing she had to a confidante was a fellow cock-tail waitress named Laura Bates. Every time she and Barbie got together, they smoked and drank and talked about how awful men were.

"What friend?" I asked.

"Emily Mills," she said, without skipping a beat. "You don't know her. I met her at the club one night. It was her birthday yesterday, so I, well, helped her celebrate."

"Did Laura go to this Emily Mills birthday party?"

"It wasn't really a party. And no. Laura doesn't really know her." She stood up and said, "I better go get dressed so I can drive you to work." I could hear her humming as she walked away.

Oddly enough, even though I knew her excuse of

having gotten together with a new friend was totally lame, I *still* wanted to believe her. After all, she was my mother. What kind of mother would look her daughter in the eye and lie?

Barbie, that's who. As soon as I picked up the newspaper my mother had been reading, I realized what a sucker I was. Smack on the front page was a picture of a prune-faced little old lady. The caption said: *Emily Mills, county's oldest woman, turns 101.*

"All right, honey," my mom said, reappearing in spandex shorts and a running bra. "We should get going. Ready?"

I set down the paper. My mom and I had gotten into fights before, and they were not pretty. They were the really messy Jerry Springer fights, with the screaming and yelling and what have you. Anything that hadn't been nailed down had been thrown (by her) in anger at least once.

"Ready," I said as enthusiastically as I could.

This time I wasn't going to fight. I was just going to get even.

Alice and I spent our lunch hour that day eating ham and Swiss sandwiches in the employee lounge, which was pretty much your typical hotel-conference-room type of venue. Alice loved brown-bagging it and made us virtually untradeable lunches. I never wanted to give away my sandwich because the crusts were usually cut off and whatever kind of meat was inside was slathered in Hellmann's Real Mayonnaise, my favorite condiment by far. The side dish was one of two things: mini tins of Herr's salted potato sticks or a super-size bag of Fritos corn chips. And to top it all off, Alice never forgot to include either a chocolate or a vanilla Hunt's Snack Pack pudding. Like I said, untradeable.

"So did you talk to your mom about the swimming lessons?" Alice asked as she wiped a huge glob of mayo off her face with her sleeve.

"Oh, they're a go," I replied.

"That's great! I'm so glad she changed her mind."

I hated the thought of lying to Alice. Therefore, I neither confirmed nor corrected her assumption that my mother had given her consent. Lying to Barbie was another matter. After all, if anyone ever had an undeniable right to go against her parent's wishes, it was me. Besides, it wasn't like I was deceiving her to do something bad. Like Alice and Keith had said, I should know how to swim.

This is about safety, I reminded myself.

"When is your first lesson?" Alice asked again.

I looked down at my pudding so I wouldn't have to look her in the eye when I said this. "I don't know."

I could hear Alice chomping on some potato sticks. "What do you mean, you don't know?"

"Well," I said, swallowing hard. "As soon as I got to work, I walked straight toward the pool, determined to up a time for a lesson. But I opened up the gate and then I . . ."

I searched for the right words as I listened to more of Alice's loud chewing. "I just stopped dead in my tracks."

"What happened?" Alice couldn't hold back a heavy sigh.

I finally looked up from my pudding. "Keith smiled at me."

Alice paused for a moment as if waiting for the clincher. "And?" she said finally.

"And that's it."

"You didn't set up a time for swimming lessons because he smiled at you?"

Truth be told, it was more than just a smile. It was a happy smile, like an "I'm so glad to see you" smile. And that threw me for a loop. Because then it wasn't just about swimming anymore. It was about him and me. Or me wanting to be with him. In fact, wanting it so bad, I felt my breath catch in my throat, and for one whole second my white plastic shoes melted into the pavement and I couldn't move. And then Keith got down from his chair and headed in my direction. So I did the only not-so-logical thing I could think of. I got out of there. Fast.

"Oh, Steffie," Alice said sadly. But she wasn't half as sad as I was. I had acted like a looney. And why? Because I obviously had some sort of chemical imbalance.

Right as I was about to spoon the entire contents of my pudding cup into my mouth, Warthog came bursting into the employee lounge and informed the staff that there was an "emergency" in the men's pool bathroom and someone needed to take care of it. Unsurprisingly, not one person volunteered.

And then I heard Alice say, "Steffie will do it."

I immediately kicked her foot. I knew exactly what she was up to.

"Great," Warthog said in relief, and then handed me a trusty plunger.

I gave Alice an evil eye as I stood up. Then I walked out of the room, plotting to spike my best friend's Mountain Dew with a huge dose of Metamucil. After all, she was sixty-something and desperately needed the fiber.

I made my way outside and down to the pool. Fortunately, it had rained that morning so the pool was pretty empty. The only lifeguard I recognized was the skinny brown-haired one who was attempting to prove his masculinity and hipness by sporting a soul patch.

I knocked on the men's bathroom door and said, "Anyone in here?"

The door opened and Keith poked his perfectly shaped head out. "Hey," he said, as if he'd been expecting me.

"Hey," I said, as my heart catapulted into my throat.

"I heard there was a mess." And then I held up my plunger as if to prove my point and reassure him that I wasn't a psycho stalker or merely someone who had adored him for exactly forty-four days and watched him through binoculars on a regular basis.

He held open the door for me gallantly and allowed me to enter. We walked inside the smelly men's room, and I followed Keith to the middle stall. In my quick, expert assessment I could tell the problem was confined to the toilet itself (thank God).

Keith took the plunger out of my hands and began plunging the toilet for me. How nice was that? I could see his triceps flexing with each plunge. How sexy was that? I couldn't stop my knees from nervously knocking together. How pathetic was that?

"So," he said. "When do you want to begin your swimming lessons?"

"Um, I don't know," I heard myself mumble.

He plunged the toilet a couple more times and then flushed it. "You haven't changed your mind, have you?" he asked, handing me back the plunger and plucking me out of my trance. His hand accidentally touched mine and I honest to God quivered.

"No," I managed to blurt out.

He smiled again. It was that same lopsided smile he had given me earlier that day.

"How about tonight after the pool closes," he said. "Nine o'clock?"

"Are you sure we won't get in trouble?" I asked, hoping Keith didn't get the double meaning.

"I wouldn't worry about it," Keith replied. He crossed his arms over his chest and grinned at me. "I've snuck into the pool plenty of times."

I wanted to say, "That's pretty dangerous for a Boy Scout," and wink at him.

But what I actually did say was "Okay," and then darted out of the bathroom.

As I walked back to the clubhouse, I tried to ignore the sense of doom that had settled in my chest. Most girls would've been ecstatic to be in my position. Unfortunately for me, I was paying attention to this stupid thing called a conscience. And as much as I had wanted to take swimming lessons without my mother's permission, a little voice in my head was saying: *Just because Barbie is being deceitful doesn't mean you have to be that way too. . . . Two wrongs don't make a right. . . . You're not responsible for Barbie's behavior but you are responsible for your own. . . . blah, blah, blah.*

Therefore, for the sake of my sanity, I had no choice but to come clean. I was going to inform Barbie of my intention to take swim lessons, and hope for the best. But that evening, the minute I walked in the door from work, Barbie greeted me with open arms, which was weird, because we Rogerses had never been keen on PDA. Still, there Barbie was, all dressed up with arms outstretched.

"Guess what?" she said, giving me a big squeeze. "My friend just called and said they had an extra ticket to the Washington symphony and wanted me to come along. Isn't that sweet?"

Apparently this mysterious friend didn't have a gender. He had become the proverbial "they" because my mother felt too guilty to lie outright and say "she" when it was really a very married "he."

"Emily Mills?" I asked. "The birthday girl?"

A quick shadow passed over her face. A slight pang of guilt. But apparently not overwhelming enough to inspire a confession.

"That's right," she said, giving me a quick peck on the cheek (obviously so discombobulated that she had already forgotten she had just given me a big hug). "Call me on my cell if you need anything."

I probably could've blurted out my intent to take a swimming lesson before she slammed the door. In retrospect, I also could've called her on her cell and told her. But instead, I kept mum. The pendulum had once again swung back, and as far as I was concerned, she didn't deserve my honesty. My conscience would just have to deal. In any case, I really didn't have time to dwell. I needed a new bathing suit. And fast.

Alice and I decided that with less than three hours to spare, the Parkfield Outlet Center was our best bet. Alice wasted no time in speeding over to get me in her giant green Cadillac. Alice was so tiny and the car was so big that she practically had to reach up just to hold the steering wheel. Her husband had bought it used back in 1988, which meant that it had been on this earth even longer than me. Because it was from Roland, it was (as Alice had said) sentimental transportation. But there was nothing sentimental about the way Alice drove, which can only be described as maniacal.

After several near crashes and a lot of obscenities, we reached our destination and began rummaging through the racks. I found a couple of bikinis for fifty percent off the sales price and headed into the dressing room with Alice to try them on.

"What do you think?" I asked Alice after trying on the first suit. It was no BCBG, but at least it had a tropical floral pattern and was butt slimming. It also, in my uneducated opinion, seemed to possess the necessary qualities of sexy but not too sexy and cute but not too cute. The only problem was the flip-flops. Alice had fixed them by wrapping duct tape around the toe thingy and under the shoe itself. Although they were still (by far) the most comfortable pair of shoes I had ever owned, I must say the duct tape screamed "I am proud white trash."

"Take your hands away from your stomach," she said as I kicked off my flip-flops. "And stand up straight."

This was one of the drawbacks of having a best friend who was old enough to be my grandmother.

She asked me things like "Did you eat a good dinner?" And reminded me to do stuff like "Stand up straight." Things that a best friend my own age would never have mentioned, probably because she would have been too busy slouching and not eating dinner.

"I'll tell you what," Alice said. "One look at you in that suit, and he's going to fall madly in love with you."

"Oh, Alice," I said with a little wave, as if that was the furthest thing from my mind.

"Steffie, it's time you realized how beautiful you are. You were always pretty, but in the past two weeks, everything has miraculously come together. Your eyes, your hair. Everything has caught up with your nose. And you're definitely losing weight around your thigh region. One look at you in that suit, and he's going to forget all about Mora."

I appreciated the sweet yet kind-of-backhanded compliment and where Alice was trying to go with all that. But quite frankly, even if "everything" had "caught up with" my nose and I was starting to look more like a banana than a pear, I would never be all-American pretty like, well, Mora Cooper.

"Let's pay for your suit and go get some dinner," Alice said. "You should eat something before your lesson."

I stood still, looking at my bikini-clad reflection in the mirror. What if Alice was right? What if Keith took one look at me in my new bikini and fell madly, crazily in love?

I sucked in my stomach and stuck out my chest as the scene unfolded in my mind. I would walk into the pool area and strike a Miss USA pose in front of the floodlights. Keith, of course, wouldn't notice me at first. Suddenly he would become aware that he was not alone. Slowly . . . very slowly . . . he would turn, and then *bang*—he would see me. His eyes would fixate on mine and his mouth would fall agape. After considerable struggle, he would regain his composure and walk slowly toward me as he said, *Stef . . . is that really you? I had no idea that you were so . . . so . . .*

"How about the Pancake House?" Alice asked, stepping in front of the mirror, strategically blocking my view.

And just like that I was back in the dressing room, listening to my stomach rumble. "Sounds good," I said.

After dinner, I put my new suit on under my clothes, and Alice drove me to the club. Even though I was doing my best to reassure myself that this whole swimming lessons thing was really no big deal, as soon as I stepped out of the car, I felt my pancake rise up and wedge itself in my esophagus.

At first glance, the pool looked completely empty. The sun had set only minutes earlier, and although it was dark, it was a hazy, soft darkness, still light enough to see clearly. It was still warm too, and the air felt kind of heavy and sticky at the same time.

Then suddenly, something occurred to me. What if Keith had forgotten? All this nervousness for nothing! It was almost laughable. And then Keith strode out of the lifeguard office in that confident yet humble way of his, and laughing was not even an option.

"I wasn't sure you'd show," he said with a hint of a smile.

Oh. My. God. Gorgeous.

"I want to learn how to swim," I said stiffly, almost like I was a robot or something.

"Good," he said, peeling off his red T-shirt.

I had always known that my infatuation with Keith was, for the most part, based on looks. This was confirmed one hundred percent when I gazed at his mesmerizing ab muscles and his taut, smooth, virtually hairless skin. Alice wouldn't have been impressed, though. She had loved that Roland was hairier than a sasquatch.

Keith nodded toward the water, as if to tell me, *Let's get on with it.*

Now it was time for me to disrobe. I hadn't thought much about how awkward that would be, but apparently the awkwardness was palpable, because Keith turned away from me and went to grab some towels. The guy was a saint. A saint in the body of an underwear model.

I slowly pulled off my shirt and shrugged off my shorts. Even though I had on my bikini underneath, I was immediately aware of how much of my skin Keith was going to see. Then I thought about how much of it he was going to touch and I nearly doubled over from stomach cramp pain.

Damn the Pancake House.

Keith dove into the deep end. He swam the length of the pool underwater and popped his head up in the shallow end. I was still gripping my stomach and hoping that Alice was right about my thighs.

"You okay?" he asked, glancing at me quickly before checking the skimmer. So much for the Miss USA moment. As he busied himself with the skimmer, I tried to put my intestinal malfunctions out of my head, walked around the pool, and dipped my toe into the lukewarm water.

"It gets warmer once you get used to it." Keith snapped the skimmer back into place and focused his deep brown eyes on me.

In a sudden burst of courage (or perhaps it was hysteria), I eased down the steps and stood directly in front of him. Beads of water were gleaming on every inch of him. He looked incredible.

"The first thing we're going to learn is how to float. So you're going to lean back and I'm going to put my arms underneath you."

This sounded so hot. "You want me to lie back?"

"Right, and I'll hold you up."

I started to arch myself backward and stopped.

Then I felt his wet hand on my waist. "Just relax."

It all sank in. I was in a pool. With Keith McKnight. Without Barbie's permission.

Whoa.

The next thing Keith did was put his hands on my shoulders, guiding me backward. I felt stiff as a board as I attempted to lie straight while he supported my back, his hands pressing hard against my bare skin. He took a step and I reacted instinctively, attempting to right myself. His grasp tightened as he said, "I'm not going to let anything happen to you. Focus on the feel of the water. And trust me."

Although Keith didn't know this, what he'd suggested was a tall order. Trust him? After every finger move, Barbie had said she wasn't going to let anything happen to me either.

I forced myself to lean backward again, resting up against him as my body bobbed on top of the water. As he began to move, pulling me with him, the water swooshed around me and I felt as though I was wrapped in a cocoon. It was as if gravity had disappeared and I was light as a feather. I felt a tickle in my stomach, the same amazing sensation I had every time I spotted Keith through Alice's binoculars. There was only one way to describe it.

I felt alive.

Without warning, Keith stopped and helped me to

my feet. "The thing to remember, Steffie, is that learning to swim has as much to do with the mind as it does the body. It's all about instincts and attitude."

Oh yeah. It sure was.

He turned around and pulled himself out of the pool. Then he grabbed a kickboard, jumped back into the water, and handed the board to me. "I want you to hold on to the board and kick across the pool."

"By myself?"

"Just hold on to the board," he repeated. "You'll do great."

Encouraged by his words, I clutched the board against me with unbridled enthusiasm. *I can do this*, I told myself. Just because my mother was terrified of the water and that I would have my own TCI, just because I had tempted fate and the love lunacy gods by taking swim lessons with my fantasy guy even though I knew my mother would jump on me like a monkey on a cupcake if she found out, did not necessarily mean I was doomed to repeat the history of those who'd gone before me. My mother's fears didn't have to be my own, right?

"Keep your arms over the top of the board. And move your legs like this," he said happily, making a scissoring motion with his legs. He seemed to be genuinely enjoying this, and it just made him even cuter. "Don't be afraid to let it rip. I want to see some really hard kicks."

Keith gave me a little push into the water. I held on to the sides of the board and began to kick. I reached the end and stopped. A surge of pride and freedom ripped through me and I turned around and smiled at Keith. He was beaming right back at me.

"Awesome, Steffie." He nodded toward the opposite side of the pool. "Keep it going." And so I shoved off again, reaching the other side and turning around. After a while, I got so good that I didn't even have to stop and stand up, I just swung my board around and kept going.

"Nice work," Keith said finally. "I think that's enough for tonight." He took my board and said, "How do you feel?"

"Good," I said.

But that was a huge understatement. I felt *great*. The combination of propelling myself through the water and accomplishing this big feat and being alone with Keith had made it one of the best nights of my life, one that I didn't want to end. I stood directly in front of him, my feet firmly planted on the bottom of the pool.

"Why don't you come back on Friday," he said. "Same time."

Then he took a piece of my hair and brushed it out of my eyes. I was almost sure it was something a boyfriend would do.

But when Keith leapt out of the pool, dripping wet and still full of energy, I remembered there was someone in his life who would definitely know for sure.

That was why I raced to the ladies' locker room and threw up my dinner.

5

Up until then, my love life could have been summed up in one word: *nada*.

As in nothing. As in no action at all. Except for the time I went to second base. But I didn't really count that because:

a) It wasn't like I was really dating the guy—I just met him at a party and he asked if I wanted to make out and I said yes.

b) The make-out session lasted about one minute and consisted of him sticking his tongue in my mouth and swirling it around like a sonic toothbrush while giving my boob a quick honk (which caused me to laugh so hard that he got all insulted and left).

c) The next day when I saw him in school, he didn't even acknowledge me.

I'd never experienced a tender moment when someone cared enough about me to brush the hair out of my eyes. Not that Keith brushing the hair out of my eyes actually meant anything.

"Alice, when I get married, will you be my maid of honor?"

It was late Friday afternoon and she and I were cleaning the tile grout in one of the ballroom lavatories. She put down her Tilex. "Steffie. He brushed your hair back. Let's not get ahead of ourselves."

"This has nothing to do with Keith," I said, throwing my scrub brush back into Alice's bucket and dashing out to the ballroom. I mean *really*. What had inspired Alice to bring up Keith? Especially considering the fact that, since I had arrived at work, I had done everything *but* talk about Keith. (I had already called Alice when I got home from my swimming lesson and described everything in detail.)

In fact, I had purposely kept the conversation light and non–Keith related. So far, we had talked about whether or not love at first sight existed (Alice didn't think so but I knew otherwise), whether it was better to marry a rich man or a poor man (no-brainer), and whether it was better to have a big wedding or small (Alice had small but I voted big). So I really didn't know what in the world Alice was talking about.

She followed me out onto the freshly waxed dance floor and stood behind me as I gazed into the wall of mirrors. Suddenly, there were twenty polyester pear girls and twenty tiny black-haired old ladies.

"I was just curious," I said, obviously annoyed.

Twenty Alices raised their eyebrows.

"*Just* curious," I repeated.

"Okay, then," she said finally. "I would be delighted to be your maid of honor."

"Traditional cake or nontraditional?" I asked, even though I already knew the answer to that. Barbie and I had discussed wedding cakes in detail (we always discussed wedding stuff when Barbie was in Barbie bliss), and we agreed that weddings and anything associated with them should be traditional. Otherwise, why bother? I always thought that it was sad that Barbie never got a wedding of her own, though. I was sure she and my dad would have gotten hitched if he hadn't been *already married!*

Alice sat down on one of the regal-looking ballroom chairs. "I'll have to think about that one."

"All weddings should have white cake." I emphasized this statement by twirling in front of the mirrors.

Alice just put her hands over her face in defeat.

A half hour later, we moved on to the dining room. The staff was prepping for the dinner rush, so the place had been closed off to Tippecanoe members a few minutes before we arrived on the scene. All the tables were empty—except for one. That was the table where

Mora's mother was holding court with all her obnoxiously dressed we're-just-as-good-as-the-Hiltons (yeah right!) friends.

Since Warthog had this dumb rule about us maids not talking in the dining room while club patrons were there, I was determined to wipe the baseboards as quickly as possible so that Alice and I could continue our fascinating bridal discussion.

She and I split up, each taking a side of the room. I was speeding along, almost to the halfway point, when I heard Mrs. Cooper's friend in the big-brimmed yellow sun hat say, "How's Mora? Is she still dating Ed's son?" (Ed was short for Edward McKnight, Keith's dad.)

My hand froze in midair—damp dirty cloth and all.

"Oh yes," Mrs. Cooper said while playing with her peach-colored Yves Saint Laurent neck scarf. (Mora was truly the spitting image of her mom.) "I have the feeling that in five years I might be planning a wedding."

Obviously Alice was aware of my distress and frozen hand, because she came over and whispered, "Why don't you start doing the club room? I'll finish in here."

But I couldn't move. My eyes were still fixed on Mora's mother as she gazed at her perfectly manicured nails.

"Five years? Mora will just be out of college," the sun-hat friend said. "Isn't that a little young to be getting married?"

"So?" Mora's mom replied. "Rick and I were college sweethearts. And Keith is a wonderful, responsible boy."

Even though Alice was tugging on my frozen hand and I knew I should leave ASAP, I still couldn't move.

"When do you leave for the beach?" the other stuffy woman with the huge tinted Dior sunglasses asked.

"Tonight, as soon as Rick gets off work. He's been assigned a case that's had him working night and day."

Suddenly Mora's mother glanced at me. *"Perdone, camarera,"* she said, shaking her iced tea glass at me. *"Más té helado, por favor."*

I was almost certain that I was delusional. "Excuse me?"

"Oh—you speak English," she said, giggling. "Well, that's refreshing, isn't it?" Then she grinned and looked around the table, waiting for the applause. Although she didn't get any applause, she did get some laughter.

"Really, Bitsy. You *are* terrible," said I-wear-my-ridiculous-sunglasses-inside woman.

"It's true, though," said sun-hat lady. "You need to speak Spanish to communicate to any of the help these days. It took twenty minutes to explain to Isabella that I wanted her to dust the blinds in my bedroom!"

At least the acknowledgment of my presence and the politically incorrect banter broke my trance. Even though it was crystal clear I wasn't her waitress, I took her glass and used the opportunity to escape into the kitchen, which is where I came face to chest with Keith.

As much as I'd wanted to play it cool and act as if I hadn't loved him for forty-six days, the sight of him was enough to make me stop breathing and cause the muscle near my right eye to twitch.

"Hi," he said. "Warthog told me I'd find you here."

I swallowed hard and finished refilling Mrs. Cooper's iced tea. "Yeah, that guy is always up my butt."

Immediately my stomach rumbled. I had just provided Keith with the image of our sweaty disgusting boss being up . . . my . . . *butt*! What was I thinking?

But instead of being grossed out, he just chuckled. "Well, I was hoping we could move our lesson to a little bit later tonight," he began, following me as I headed back out into the dining room.

"Keith!" Mora's mother exclaimed as she saw him. "We were just talking about you."

Keith flashed her a quick smile but kept his attention focused on me.

"Can we make it nine-thirty instead?" he asked me.

"Um, not really," I said, stopping. I really didn't want to have this conversation in front of Mrs. Cooper. She would definitely sense something amiss and go running back to Mora, and that would be so not good.

"All right," he said with a shrug. "We'll keep it at nine."

"No," I said, looking around for Alice. Where had she gone? "I'm sorry . . . I can't make it tonight," I said firmly. And then I turned and headed out as fast as I could in search of Alice. After running around Tippecanoe for a good twenty minutes, I found her in the weirdest place—sitting on a bench between the shower and the sauna in an empty ladies' locker room.

"Oh my God, Alice, I just told Keith I couldn't make my lesson tonight." I plopped down next to her.

She wiped some sweat off her brow with a towel and heaved another heavy sigh. "Jesus Christ, Steffie. Why'd you do that for?"

"I know, I'm a moron." I leaned forward to quell the rampant stomach pain that had come back to haunt me. "I ran into him when I went to get Mora's mom more tea." Then I realized the glass of iced tea was still in my hand. I really was a moron.

"Ah, now I understand," Alice said sarcastically.

"Well, what can I say? I guess I freaked out about the whole him-marrying-Mora thing. You know, after they both go to college and . . . like . . . sing in the glee club together."

"Really, Steffie, I wouldn't pay attention to anything that came out of Bitsy Cooper's mouth," Alice said with a snort. "Honestly, I've known her from the day she was born and I can tell you this much: she doesn't know her ass from a hole in the ground."

Speaking of asses, I was about to tell Alice about my lame comment to Keith when she started coughing uncontrollably.

"Alice?" I said. "Are you all right?"

She managed to stop long enough to smile. "Yeah,

must be residue from those thousand packs of cigarettes I smoked in the eighties. It'll pass."

I handed her Mora's mother's iced tea. "Here, try drinking this."

"You don't think she has herpes, do you?" Alice held the glass up to the fluorescent light, as if she was trying to spot any communicable diseases.

"I doubt it," I said, grinning. "She probably has her Spanish-speaking maid dry-clean her lips."

Alice downed the iced tea and closed her eyes again as she took some deep breaths. "You know what would make us feel better?" she asked quietly. "A list of how many plastic surgery procedures Bitsy's had."

Then she put her arm around me, pulled me in for a hug, and we both sat there for a while, giggling like best friends do.

I arrived home from work around six-thirty. I heated up a package of minipizzas, yanked open a new bag of M&M's, rummaged through the dirty-clothes hamper for my favorite Hawaiian board shorts and white tank top, and settled in for a long interruption-free night of TV. My night had immediately brightened when I was lucky enough to score an *AFHV* marathon on ABC Family. After six episodes of hilarity, I had finished the pizza and the package of M&M's and was brushing my teeth when the phone rang.

I answered the phone with a mouthful of toothpaste. "Yep?" I mumbled in my best annoyed voice.

"Stef? This is Keith."

Still holding the phone to my ear, I ran to the sink and spit out the toothpaste. (Actually, it was more like barfing than spitting.)

"Hello? Stef?"

I suddenly realized I hadn't even said hello yet. "Uh . . . h-hi," I stammered.

"I got your number from the employee directory. I hope you don't mind me calling," he said.

Keith could have gotten my number from an Internet porn site and I still wouldn't have minded him calling.

"It's nice to hear from you," I warbled.

"Listen, I wanted to ask you something."

"Okay," I said nervously, hoping that the next words out of his mouth would be "Will you marry me?" It was a stretch, but somehow at the time anything seemed possible.

"Are you taking these swim lessons because of me?" he asked.

It felt as though every particle in my body was about to combust.

"Um . . . no," I replied unconvincingly.

"I don't want you to feel pressured, though. Just because I think you should learn how to swim doesn't mean that you have to. And honestly, if your heart isn't in it and you'd rather be doing something else, like hanging out with your boyfriend or whatever, then it will just be a big waste of your time."

I couldn't wipe the grin off my face. For one, Keith was being so sweet that I could barely stand it. Up until then, I'd only daydreamt about talking to him on the phone, and suddenly, it was happening and he was even nicer than I had imagined. For two, he had the TV blaring so loudly in the background, it was actually a little hard to hear him—how great was that? For three, he thought I was good enough to have a boyfriend, which I was, only the boy in question should have been him.

"I really want to learn how to swim, Keith. I was just busy tonight." My voice cracked a bit, and I winced.

Keith kind of chuckled, which seemed odd. I hadn't said anything funny. "That's cool. What were you up to?"

I walked out into the messy living/dining/TV room and eyed the TV. *This* was my idea of busy? But before I could make up a good story, I realized something. The sound coming from Keith's end of the line was completely matching up with the visual from my TV.

Holy crap.

We were both watching *America's Funniest Home Videos*!

I heard Keith stifle another chuckle. Oh my God, this was unbelievable.

"Sorry, Stef. There's this marathon on ABC Family," Keith said through his charming laugh.

"I know. I'm watching it too!" I chimed in, unable to hide my enthusiasm.

"Really?"

I couldn't believe what I was about to say. "This is my favorite show of all time."

"I'm totally with you," he agreed. "Which host do you like better? That dude from *Full House* or Daisy Fuentes and her dorky male sidekick?"

I pinched myself really hard, just to make sure I wasn't hallucinating. "There's no comparison. Bob Saget is God."

Had I just said Bob Saget was God?

Apparently Keith thought my remark was off-the-wall too, because he laughed again. "You know what? I'm having a party tomorrow night. You should come and hang out."

My particles finally combusted. "Tomorrow night?"

"Yeah. My dad and his wife are going out of town so I'm having some friends over."

"Okay," I said through a gigantic grin.

"Great," he replied. "Mora and her crew aren't going to be around either, so I hope you don't mind being in the girl minority."

Whoa. No Mora.

"I live at 715 Tulare Stre—"

"I know where you live," I interrupted. "Across the creek from Alice."

The thought of Mora not being around to chaperone

Keith had obviously affected my common sense, or else I wouldn't have said something that made me sound like a psychopath.

"Right," he said after a brief hesitation. "So I'll see you tomorrow. Around seven?"

I caught a glimmer of my reflection in the TV. I may not have looked anything like my mother, but I had her plastic smile on my face.

"See you then," I answered.

After I hung up the phone, I turned off the TV. Only then did I notice that I was humming.

6

The first thought that entered my mind when my head hit the pillow was this: Telling Keith that I would come over to *his house* when Mora wasn't around to act as a buffer had been a colossal mistake. It was like I had agreed to walk into the lion's den of love lunacy holding a rack of lamb. Was I completely out of my mind?

On the other hand, I couldn't get rid of this series of thoughts either: Did Keith invite me to this party because he liked me-liked me (girlfriend potential) or just liked me (only wanted to be friends)? Even though I knew that chances were overwhelmingly good that he just liked me, what would I do if it turned out that he actually liked me-liked me?

After tossing and turning for what seemed like hours, I finally followed Alice's advice and made a list of all the scenarios that were floating inside my head:

Possibilities:

1) I walk into Keith's house only to discover I *am* the party. It is just the two of us. He has planned a romantic evening to confess his love.
2) There are other people there, all of whom suddenly treat me with a great amount of respect. He takes me by the hand and introduces me before whisking me away to a private room where we make out.
3) Keith French-kisses me and then he confesses his love.

Ugh. I was hopeless.

It was two a.m. I had just finished making my list and switched off the light when I heard Barbie's key turn in the lock. Even though most of the time Barbie was a model of instability, she still showed some elements of traditional maternal instinct. And her bedtime ritual was an example of this. Every night before she went to bed, she came into my room and kissed me goodnight. Usually I pretended to be asleep (even if I wasn't). But this time, when she leaned over to give me a peck on the forehead, my eyes were wide open.

"Oh, Jesus!" She jumped back and put her hand on her heart. "You scared me. I didn't expect you to be awake."

"I can't sleep," I announced.

"Anything going on, or are you just not tired?"

"I was invited to a party." I couldn't get this out of my mind so I figured I might as well share it with Barbie. Besides, she hadn't been this interested in me in days.

"Really?" she asked, excited. She hesitated as the hope faded from her eyes. "A young persons' party?" she asked suspiciously.

"It's the whole Mora Cooper crowd," I said. I couldn't tell her exactly who because she might recognize Keith's name. And then she might just wonder about those swimming lessons. And then I'd be screwed.

My mother's eyes lit up. "No wonder you can't sleep," she said.

I knew what she was thinking. This was my big break, the one she'd been waiting for. Her daughter would *finally* be popular. "It's not Mora herself," I said. "Just one of her friends from school." I was proud that I had managed to muster up a fraction of honesty.

"We'll have to get you something to wear!" she exclaimed.

My mother thought in terms of practicality. And no one could dispute that the woman had style. She always said her fashion sense was a remnant from her college days at UCLA, when she was getting her business degree while taking fashion design classes on the side. (That's what she was doing when she met my dad.)

When my mom got pregnant, my dad left his wife, but he died (heart attack) before his divorce was final (i.e., no moolah for Barbie or me). So, like a heroine in one of those sappy Lifetime Movie Network flicks she loved so much, Barbie had to drop out of UCLA and give up her dream of helming her own fashion empire.

In any case, I was determined to take advantage of her expertise and forget (temporarily) my grievances with her so I could enjoy our rare mother-daughter outing. And I could tell that Barbie was equally determined because she gave me a kiss and a quick nod as if confirming the deal. The knowledge that my mom was going to be involved in the preparations for my potential big night provided enough comfort that I eventually fell asleep.

The next morning my mother and I awoke and began our journey with tight smiles and curt politeness. We both did our best to veer away from any subject that might cause trouble, which meant that we spent half the thirty-minute drive to St. Michaels saying things like "There sure is lots of traffic for a Saturday!" and "Wonder when this heat is supposed to break?" We arrived at this quaint little boutique called Zip, and Barbie whizzed through the sale rack as if she'd just downed twelve cans of Red Bull. We walked out of the store twenty minutes later with a microminiskirt and an asymmetrical off-the-shoulder top—both for Barbie.

About ten specialty shops later, we finally found an outfit that I could deal with—a fancy black tank with a little ruffle around the edges, and long lean white pants. My mother shelled out the money for the clothes and we walked to Barbie's favorite restaurant, called Lila's, a cozy little coffee shop in the center of town. I ordered the California chicken sandwich. (That's what I always ordered, except for the one time when I ordered the Mediterranean chicken salad. Big mistake.)

"So I wonder which boys will be at the party," Barbie said, after she had placed her order for a Cobb salad (minus bacon, minus cheese, extra chicken, dressing on side) and we had settled into a table near the window. She and I loved watching passersby and making up stories about who they were and where they were going. Too bad Barbie was homed in on me instead of the tall guy at the parking meter out front. He was seriously H-O-T. "Who's hosting this again? A friend of Mora's?"

Uh-oh. This was bad news. As I said before, I'd never been much of a liar. And I didn't really want to mention Keith, because that would be a major red flag. "One of the lifeguards," I said, avoiding her eyes.

"Oh—so that's why the Mora Cooper crowd will be there."

My mom took a bite of her salad before dropping the bombshell. "She's dating that lifeguard who offered you the swimming lessons. Keith McKnight, right?"

I felt my stomach lurch. The server set my sandwich in front of me, but I wasn't hungry anymore.

Just then my mom's cell phone rang. She glanced at the number, and her face lit up. She looked at me and said quickly, "I'll be right back."

After Barbie went in search of a private place with good reception to talk to her married man, I looked at her empty seat and felt the same horror any daughter would feel watching her mother purposely lie down in front of an oncoming train or stick her tongue on a frozen monkey bar at the school playground. Even though I wasn't one to wallow in self-pity, I figured I was due. In an effort to cheer myself up, I decided to take a tip from Alice and make a list. I grabbed a red crayon off a nearby table and wrote on my napkin:

Things that are crappy:

> Great tank top, but no boobs
> Barbie/love lunacy
> Keith/Mora
> Me/love lunacy?

But there was one thing missing. And so I added:

> Dad

Even though he'd died before I was born, I still thought about him at times like this, times when I felt like everything just sucked. If he hadn't died, I think my life would have been extremely different. Not that I thought that Barbie would've actually married him and gotten a house in the suburbs and stuff, but I was pretty sure I would've had a much more normal life. He and Barbie would have been divorced and I would have been shuttled back and forth between the two of them. He never would have condoned Barbie's moving me across the state every year, nor would he have condoned her parading around with married boyfriends. If he had lived, I would have had a sane, stable person (besides Alice) that I could have talked to about all the important things in my life.

I glanced up just as Barbie came back into the dining room. I tossed the napkin with my list back onto my lap as she took her seat.

"You didn't have to wait for me," she said, motioning toward my untouched food.

"Oh," I said, realizing I had forgotten all about my lunch. I took a bite of my sandwich and set it back down on my plate. "Was my dad Hispanic?" I asked, between chews.

"What?" she said, visibly startled. "Why in the world would you ask a thing like that?"

"Just wondering," I said with a shrug. I swallowed.

"Mora's mother thought I looked Hispanic or Spanish or something."

"I, well, no. He wasn't."

"What was he?"

Barbie started to gaze around the room. "He was . . . American."

"I mean, what was his background? You know, his ethnicity."

"I honestly don't know," she said with a huff. "We never discussed it."

I focused back on my sandwich, annoyed. Not that I had expected Barbie to suddenly be a wealth of information, but I hadn't thought she would be this evasive. She couldn't throw me a little bone and give me some background info on my heritage?

As if reading my reaction, Barbie said, "I told you, Steffie, we were only together for about three months when I found out I was pregnant. He died shortly thereafter." She shrugged. "He wasn't in my life that long."

"Was he rich?" I asked.

"What's going on?" Barbie asked. "Why all the questions?"

"I'm just curious, that's all. You never talk about him."

She sighed long and deep as if pondering my request. Finally she said, "He was very . . . well off, yes."

"How rich? Like, Jones Island rich? Or movie-star rich?"

"Steffie, what's the point of this?"

"I'm just curious as to what kind of house we'd have if he was alive."

"Who knows?" she replied. "Maybe we'd be living right where we are." But I could tell from the look on her face that she didn't really believe what she'd said.

"Maybe your store would've taken off and we'd be millionaires," I muttered.

She forced a smile. "You know what I just decided? I'm going to rearrange my schedule so I can be home tonight and help you get ready. That way I can drive you to the party."

This was Barbie's way of distracting me. "Okay," I said.

There was an awkward silence as we both focused on our food.

"I like spending time together," Barbie said suddenly, as if half trying to convince herself. "In no time at all, you'll be graduating from high school. And then you'll be leaving me."

Then she got really quiet and she said, "I can't imagine my life without you, Steffie."

And her saying that, I decided, was the most annoying thing that had happened to me all day.

7

One of the things I adored about Alice was her unforgettable words of wisdom: "Even a dog knows the difference between being stumbled over and being kicked." This was another one of her jewels: "Promises, like piecrusts, are easily broken."

Translation: even though I did kind of believe that Barbie loved me, the only reason she'd said that thing about not being able to imagine life without me was because she was feeling guilty. Because she knew that even though she had promised to stay home on Saturday night and help me get ready for my party, she would dump me in a flash if her boyfriend called. Which was where the piecrust proverb fit in.

This was precisely why I found the whole sentiment thing annoying. If that made me mean, so be it. According to Alice, if you run with wolves, you have to howl. And like it or not, living with Barbie was like being chained to a wolf. But still, *still,* I was surprised at about three o'clock that afternoon, when Barbie and I were lying out in the sun (I usually didn't do this, but I wanted to get tan before my party) and her phone rang. I knew it was her boyfriend because after the Ludwig ring, she took it into the house.

When she came back out, she said, "Steffie, I'm sorry. But I need to go."

"Go where?"

"Out with a friend."

"Who?"

"Look, Steffie. I'm sorry, I am. But I'll make it up to you. Okay?"

But I didn't want her to make it up to me. I wanted her to do what she had promised.

"Maybe Alice can take you to the party," my mom said, which just made the whole thing even worse. I stormed into the house, went into my room, and began slamming my dresser drawers. I pulled out a T-shirt and tossed it over my head.

Barbie followed me like a heat-seeking missile. "Look," she said angrily. "It's not like I haven't done anything for you. I bought you new clothes and took you out to lunch. And this is the thanks I get? A temper tantrum? Grow up, Steffie."

Now she had gone too far. *Grow up?* And then I said it. "Emily Mills is a hundred and one years old."

My mom glanced at me.

"You lied right to my face." I waited for a response. At the very least, I thought I was owed an apology.

"What do you want me to say?" Barbie asked. Then she shook her head and sat down on my bed as if defeated.

Her surrender took me off guard. It wasn't like Barbie to throw in the towel so soon. "I want you to apologize," I replied.

"I'm sorry," she said. "I know what you're thinking, Stef, and maybe this is unfair of me to ask of you, but you need to give me a chance here."

A *chance?* "What are you talking about?"

"This situation may seem familiar, but it's not."

I rolled my eyes. "But he's married."

"Not happily. He's going to leave his wife. He hasn't been happy for a long time."

Information overload. I couldn't take it anymore, so I turned on my stereo, grabbed a copy of *Us Weekly*, and began looking for the "Stars: They're Just Like Us" section.

And then she said the words I had been waiting for: "This guy is different, Steffie. He's not like the rest. He really loves me. He's even talking about giving me the money to open that store I've been talking about. Today we're going to look at potential sites for it."

I turned up the volume, ignoring her. Eventually my mom got the message and went into her room to get ready. When she came back out, she was decked out in full mistress gear: high heels along with the tight miniskirt and the asymmetrical boob-revealing shirt she'd bought today. She kissed my forehead and said, "Have fun at your party, okay?"

"Spending the night?" I nodded toward the Adidas duffel in her hand.

"No."

"What's in the bag, then?"

She paused for a moment. "Don't wear those old flip-flops of yours tonight. Wear those cute pink ones of mine instead."

"No thanks," I barked. I flipped another page in the magazine so hard I gave myself a paper cut.

Out of the corner of my eye, I could see her bite her lip. She looked like she was about to speak, and then she shook her head and walked out without saying good-bye. After she left, I turned off my stereo and started to get dressed.

I did everything I could to not think about my mother. She had her life. If she was determined to ruin it, then so be it. What could I do?

I only had control over *me*. Wasn't that what all the headshrinks said? I put on the sexpot outfit Barbie had so carefully chosen and brushed my hair. Then I flicked on some of Barbie's mascara and some sparkly strawberry lip gloss, and reluctantly put on her cute pink shoes. And then I went into the living room and turned on the TV. As I watched a preview for a show about circus animals that was airing that night, I felt a little sad. As in, I kind of wished I hadn't had anything going on that night so I could just stay home in my oversize clothes and watch the show.

What was wrong with me?

I should have been bouncing off the walls! I had been in love with Keith McKnight for forty-seven days! He was the coolest guy around and he had *personally* invited me to his party at *his* house. His girlfriend was out of town! And he had brushed the hair out of my eyes like he was into me or something. All of that mattered way more than Barbie's new case of love lunacy. Right?

I willed myself off the couch and forced myself to turn off the TV. Then I stepped outside into the blistering ninety-five-degree heat and began walking. A half hour later, I was covered in sweat and my mascara was dripping down my face. But it didn't matter. Because I had reached my destination, and it wasn't Keith's house.

Although Keith's house was only about a hundred yards away.

"What are you doing here?" Alice asked as she sat in her gliding rocking chair, drinking a Mountain Dew and doing a Sudoko puzzle. Her black hair was wet and set in tiny rollers. She was wearing a pink sleeveless terry-cloth "housecoat" (which was just another term for bathrobe) and the fuzzy purple slippers I'd given her for her birthday.

This was another drawback to having a best friend who was old enough to be my grandma. She couldn't go to Keith's party. If she'd been my age, I would've made her go with me. And then I would've gone. Really.

8

One of the great things about Alice was that she kept her kitchen stocked with the ingredients for chocolate chip cookies. As she said, you just never knew when there might be an emergency. And me showing up on her doorstep in my new party outfit, ranting about my mother when I was supposed to be at Keith's party, was an emergency. So Alice responded accordingly, immediately turning on the silly circus TV show and whipping up a batch of raw cookie dough. We then grabbed the binoculars and planted ourselves on her lopsided sofa in front of the window so that we could have the best of both worlds: we could watch TV while experiencing Keith's party (without actually having to attend). As we took turns using the binoculars, I carefully explained to Alice why I hadn't gone. In a nutshell: I had no earthly idea.

"You were just nervous," Alice said, eating a spoonful of dough. "And having your mom leave you high and dry like that, well, it threw you for a loop. But it's okay. There'll be other parties."

"Tell that to Barbie. She's going to go nuts when she finds out I didn't go. She thinks this was my big break."

"Big break for what?"

"To be popular."

"Oh, please." Alice rolled her eyes. "It's a party. And from the looks of it," she said, as she trained the binoculars on Keith's kitchen, "not a very good one." She handed me the binoculars. "Pizza from Romero's? Yuck."

I twisted around to get a better view of the kitchen. We had been watching the house for the past hour, and with the setting of the sun and the turning on of lights (his), our view had improved dramatically. The back of Keith's house was almost all floor-to-ceiling windows, so Alice and I could see inside with all the clarity of HDTV. Suddenly, I saw Keith walk into the kitchen. Although my heart skipped a beat at the sight of him, I was almost immediately distracted by the miniskirted big-busted girl hanging on his arm and looking at him like an affectionate puppy. As I watched the girl silently jabber away, Keith stopped in front of the window and turned toward the water. I focused the binoculars back on him, and for one brief, terrible moment, it looked as if he was staring right at me. I rolled off the couch and hit the floor.

"What?" Alice asked, ducking down with me.

"Keith," I whispered. "It looked like he saw me."

Alice peeked over the couch. "Nah. The only way he could see you is if we were all lit up and he happened to have a pair of binoculars handy."

"Who's that girl with him?" I handed Alice the binoculars as I crawled back up onto the sofa.

"I don't know," Alice said, scanning the house. "I didn't get a chance to see her. They're not in the kitchen anymore and I don't know where they've gone."

"What are all those girls doing over there, anyway?" I was trying to ignore the jealousy that was sitting like a lump in my belly. "I thought I was going to be the girl minority."

Alice leaned forward for a better look. "You mean the girls watching TV in the library? Tammy Cheskus and Michelle Ronsaville. They were in Keith's class at Brucker's. They haven't been around much this summer because they both did internships out of state. But they're no threat." Alice handed me back the binoculars.

"I wish you could've seen that girl with Keith," I said, hoping at one point Alice would recognize her and tell me she was his long-lost sister.

"Look, Steffie, are you sure you don't want me to take you over there? I could watch through my binoculars and you could give me a code or something if you wanted me to come and get you."

I turned back toward the TV. "I'd rather be here. If I

was at Keith's, I never would've seen that dog jumping through the burning hoop."

"That *was* cute," Alice admitted.

"Besides, how can I go to a party when Barbie's in the third stage of love lunacy?"

"So what? Why let your mom's love lunacy get in the way of you having a good time?"

"My point is that I'm going to be moving soon anyway. So why bother expending all that effort to make new friends? It hardly seems worth the trouble."

"I think Keith is worth the trouble, don't you?"

I picked some chocolate chips out of the dough and popped them into my mouth. "Let's face it. Keith wanting to hook up with me is about as unlikely as me winning the hot-dog-eating contest at the county fair. I mean, even if he wanted to cheat on Mora, he would do what all cheaters do: he would pick a girl like Barbie, a hot tamale who goes on dates armed with a duffel bag stuffed with lingerie." Actually, a girl just like the big-boobed miniskirted one that had been hanging on his arm.

I twisted around once again and focused the binoculars on his house. "I wish we could see his bedroom from here," I said.

"You don't think he took that girl you saw him with up to his room, do you?" Alice asked.

"I don't know," I said. "I hope not."

"I'm sure he didn't . . . but if it would make you feel better, I bet we could see his room from the Berkensteins' dock," Alice said. She stood up and grabbed another spoonful of the cookie dough. She swallowed it and grinned mischievously. "Come on."

"But what if someone sees us?" I asked. After all, the Berkensteins' dock jutted so far out into the creek that a long jumper could make it to Keith's back door without getting wet.

"He's not going to see us," Alice said. "The dock is totally dark. And besides, Keith is inside."

I followed Alice out the door and around the side of the house. We went down to the dock and crept out to the end. I trained the binoculars on the second floor of his house. "Where's his room?" I whispered.

"Over there." Alice pointed to a dark window. Just then, I heard a door slam. "Let's go check out the boat," I heard a girl giggle from Keith's backyard. I could only assume the boat she was referring to was the one directly in front of us, the one roped to the end of Keith's parents' dock.

"Oh, crap," I heard Alice say. She stepped backward, inadvertently setting off the motion control on the dock lights. Suddenly, Alice and I were illuminated as if onstage.

"Let's get out of here!" she exclaimed, and grabbed my arm. We both turned and ran as fast as we could (which was not very, thanks to Alice's slippers) back up the dock and into the darkness, practically diving behind a large bush in the corner of the Berkensteins' yard. We crouched down as Alice peeked around the bush, scanning the perimeter with her binoculars.

"Do you think they saw us?" I panted.

"Nope," Alice replied. She gave me the binoculars and I peered through the lens just in time to see Keith's hussy climb onto the back of his parents' boat.

"That's the girl," I whispered, handing the binoculars back to Alice.

"Rebecca Lipton," Alice explained. "She's Keith's aunt."

"His aunt? She's kind of young to be his aunt."

"She's his mother's younger sister. She's only seven years older than Keith."

"Wow," I said. "Weird."

"Yeah," Alice agreed. She put the binoculars down and looked at me. And suddenly I was hit by the ridiculousness of it all: Alice in her curlers, robe, and slippers and me in my brand-new outfit, hiding behind a bush in the Berkensteins' yard, spying on Keith McKnight while discussing the age of his aunt. And if that wasn't weird, I didn't know what was.

I started to laugh, and Alice followed suit, guffawing so hard that I had to grab her to prevent her from falling over. "Oh, Steffie," she said. "Even though you should've gone to that party, I'm really glad you didn't."

Early Sunday morning, I woke up to my landline ringing. I didn't even bother checking the caller ID because

I was pretty sure it was Alice calling to ask me if I had any plans for the day and whether or not I was going to redeem myself with Keith for skipping out on his party. I was half-asleep when I picked up, so my "hello" sounded more like a "hur-mrph."

"Steffie?"

Oh, crap. It wasn't Alice. It was . . . *Keith*.

"Hi!" I managed to immediately perk myself up.

"I have some free time and was wondering if you wanted to come to the club for a quick lesson."

He said it just like that. Like I had never canceled my second swim lesson or stood him up at his party.

"I'll be right there," I said, hanging up the phone.

Then my mother walked into the room wearing her bathrobe and holding a large mug of piping hot coffee. She looked like she'd barely slept an hour.

"Who was that?" she asked.

"I have to go to the club," I said.

"On your day off?"

I shrugged, determined not to lie. If push had come to shove, I would've told her the truth. Honest.

"They can wait until you have some breakfast," my mom said coolly, as if she had a whole spread waiting for me in the kitchen, instead of the open box of Froot Loops I knew was sitting on the table.

"No," I said, pulling my maid uniform out of the dirty clothes hamper. "*They* want me to come right over." (Notice the flexible gender use.)

I put my maid uniform on (yes, this was a tad deceitful) and rode my bike to the club. The fresh morning air felt so good as it breezed by my face. The sun hadn't been out too long, but the temperature couldn't have been milder or more inviting. It was as if some higher power was trying to convince me that the day was about opportunity and second chances. All I had to do was make the most of it.

When I arrived at Tippecanoe, I saw Keith beside the pool and gave him a quick wave before going into the dressing room and changing into my suit. It was then that I realized I hadn't showered that morning. I took a whiff of my armpits and thanked the Masters of the Universe for giving me the ability to smell my own BO. I jumped into the shower and scrubbed myself with a teeny leftover bar of Ivory soap. Before I headed out to the pool, I checked myself out in the mirror. Surprisingly enough, the wet look didn't appear too bad on me. Then I took a deep breath and strode out of the locker room.

But when I reached the deck of the pool, it was not Keith waiting for me, but Mora.

She raised an eyebrow, obviously surprised to see me standing before her all wet and in my bikini.

I gasped and instinctively crossed my arms over my bare belly. What was she doing there, anyway? Wasn't she supposed to be out of town? And most important, weren't the gods supposed to be on my side?

"She's your swim lesson?" Mora said, her voice heavy with displeasure.

"Yep," Keith said from behind me.

"How long will you be?" she asked Keith. " 'Cause I can wait."

"If this is a bad time," I said, turning around to meet Keith's amazing gaze, "we can reschedule."

He glared at Mora. "You go on ahead," he said. "I'll meet up with you when I'm finished."

"I don't mind waiting," she whined. It was weird, hearing Mora sound desperate. I almost felt sorry for her. Almost.

"We can do this another time," I repeated to Keith.

"Get in the water, Stef," Keith said, handing me a kickboard. "Start doing laps across the shallow end."

He then took Mora gently by the arm and led her toward the gate.

This was one of those moments in which bionic hearing would have been useful. As it was, with all my splashing and what have you, I couldn't hear a word. But from what I could see, Mora looked really upset. This was definitely not something I wanted to admit to myself at that moment, but I knew more than anyone how love lunacy could tear at the fabric of happiness. Here was some more evidence slapping me in the face.

After a brief discussion, Mora finally left and Keith dove into the water. It was one of those perfect dives, nice and sleek, with the legs together and toes pointed.

He swam the length of the pool underwater and popped up beside me, his hair slicked back and his eyes wide.

I stood up and handed him my kickboard. He gave me a little smile. "Sorry about that," he said, with a glance in Mora's direction.

"It's okay," I said.

He looked at me really intensely, as if I had just spoken a different language and he was trying to interpret what I had said. Finally, he said, "Why don't you turn on your back and we'll practice floating again."

I leaned backward until I felt his hands supporting me from underneath. He was staring down at me and his face looked incredible, even when it was inverted. Maybe it was the light (the sun was still rising in the sky), but there was some sort of sparkle in his eyes. Whatever the look was, I liked it, much more than I should have. Just like I liked the way his skin felt against mine and the way he said my name.

"So what happened to you last night, Steffie?" he asked.

I froze and my feet sank to the bottom like dead weight as I stood up again. "Well, something came up."

He gave a curt nod, as if he thought I was blowing him off or something. "Let's try it again."

For a moment, I thought he was talking about his party. As in, "Let's try it again. I'll invite you, and this time you show up." But then I realized he just wanted me to float again, and my stomach began to cramp.

"This time I'm going to take my hands away," Keith said. "Just relax and keep your arms spread out."

The wind picked up and a chill raced over me. "I'll sink."

"Not if you relax," he said. I leaned backward until I felt his strong hands. "It's all mental, Stef," he was saying. "You need to believe you can do it. You need to conquer your fear."

I closed my eyes and kept repeating those words in my head.

He took away one hand and then the other. I felt a surge of pride as I realized I was on top of the water, floating all by myself. And then I thought, *What if I drown?*

And then I sank.

Keith scooped me back up and said, "You all right?"

I coughed up the water I had swallowed. Who (besides me) drowned in the shallow end? "I'm fine," I said.

"You lost your concentration," he said. "This time I'll hold you up until I think you're ready."

I tried really hard to relax. I tried to pretend that the hottest guy in the world was not standing beside me, staring down at me with those gorgeous brown eyes while his hands practically caressed my bare skin. Instead I imagined myself at Alice's house, sitting on her slightly lopsided IKEA couch, covered up in the afghan she'd made herself, watching reality TV.

And after a while, I realized that Keith had removed

his hands and I was not only breathing rhythmically, I was floating. I bobbed away, just lying there, looking up at the brightening sky.

"You did it," he said excitedly.

I stood up and grinned. As he looked at me, I felt as though he could see right through me.

Keith looked at his waterproof sports watch and scowled. "Sorry, Stef. I have to go."

I could feel my face tighten as I tried to hold my smile. But it didn't work. I knew I was frowning. I knew he was going to meet Mora.

"Can we meet again tomorrow?" he asked.

"I'd love to," I said meekly. "But I can't. I told Alice I'd help her mow her lawn. Her back is out or something like that."

"Really? Well, I'll come by after work and do it." His eyes were glowing again.

"You don't h-have to do that," I stammered. "I can handle it."

Keith chuckled and lightly gripped my upper arm. "I know you can, Stef. Check out these muscles."

Holy Cheesy Nacho Hamburger Helper. What was *that*?

"Actually, we have a big riding mower that we hardly ever use." He grinned. "It'll be much easier this way. And besides, I want you to save your strength for me."

With that, Keith hopped out of the pool. Streams of

water dripped off his long legs and his swim trunks, which were hanging so low that I got a quick look at the upper part of his left butt cheek.

Minutes later, I dried off, tucked my suit into a Ziploc bag, and changed back into my uniform. I rode my bike home, humming so loudly I was practically singing. I just couldn't help myself.

"Back so soon?" my mother asked. For once, she was not sitting in front of the TV watching some washed-up B-list actress like Connie Selleca (aka Mrs. John Tesh) grapple with her daughter's cracked-out pimp. Instead she was doing something incredibly bizarre. She was sitting at the kitchen table painting a large oyster shell. Yep, my mother was entertaining herself with *arts and crafts*.

"What are you doing?" I was certain that my eyes were deceiving me.

"Oh," she said with a little laugh. "I saw a shell like this when I was with my *friend*, and so I thought I'd make one for *them* to remember our day. That's all."

Translation: she was painting a shell for her married boyfriend. How Martha-esque was that? But I didn't say anything. Instead, I went into my room and changed back into my pajamas. I brushed my teeth and climbed into bed. It was Sunday morning at nine a.m. After all, I had the whole day to contemplate how I was rapidly going through the initial stages of love lunacy, and berate myself accordingly. I thought I should get an early start on it.

Barbie came into my room and sat on the edge of my bed. She looked almost worried about me. "Stef," she said. "I just want you to know that I love you. You know that, right? You're the most important thing in my life."

I definitely did not want to have this conversation with my mom. Not then. And so I decided to ignore the need I felt to point out that I wasn't really flattered to hear that I was the most important thing in her life. For one, she had already dumped me twice for this Ludwig guy. For two, besides her '99 red Malibu, she really didn't have that many things to write home about. No other family. No real friends. Just the occasional married man. So what was she really saying? That she loved me more than this guy she had been dating for a couple of weeks?

"It's not easy being a mom," she continued. "Especially a single one."

And that's when I saw it. Considering the size, I was actually surprised that I hadn't noticed it before. "You're wearing a new ring," I said. It was gold and sparkly, encrusted with diamonds.

"Oh," she said, stretching out her hand and admiring it. "Yes." She smiled and sighed. "My friend is, well, very generous."

Normally this would've been my breaking point. I would've jumped out of bed and listed all the gifts she had received from all her men and pointed out that none of these relationships had ever amounted to anything more than a move across the state. Instead I kept my mouth shut and closed my eyes really tight as I tried to remember how it felt to float.

"I've made some mistakes. I know I have," my mom said softly. "But you need to give me a break here. You're not my mother, Stef. You're my daughter. And you need to respect my decisions. And you need to trust me. I'm going to make a better life for us, Steffie. I promise."

I was on top of the water, just bobbing along.

And it worked, it really worked.

Then Barbie said this: "So how was the party last night? Did you have fun?"

I pictured Keith's brilliant smile and the cute dimple on his chin and the way he said, "You just have to believe you can do it." For some reason, it felt okay to lie.

"Yes, Mom. Everything was great."

9

Alice (and other Tippecanoe Country Club employees) had a favorite saying: "A trip to Mr. Warthog's office is like a trip to the dentist." Meaning it was unpleasant and you felt crappy afterward. (Most of the employees at Tippecanoe had bad teeth.)

There was only one reason why an employee was asked to Warthog's office midseason: to be fired. So even though I went to work on Monday morning in a love-lunacy-style schizoid mood (I had spent all of Sunday vacillating between these two thoughts: *I love Keith McKnight* and *I hate myself*), my mood was made even more not-so-fabulous when Mr. Warthog summoned me to his office. And it was made still worse by the fact that, when I opened the door, I saw that my mother was waiting for me too.

"Come in," Mr. Warthog said, waving me in and motioning for me to take a seat next to Barbie.

Barbie's legs were nervously bouncing up and down.

Her arms were crossed in front of her chest and she gave me one of her nasty "You're in big trouble" stares.

"Stef," Mr. Warthog said. "I just got through explaining to your mother that a member has filed an official complaint regarding you. Apparently you were using the club pool when it was closed to the public. That is against Tippecanoe rules."

Translation: Mora had ratted me out. Warthog had told my mother, who, unbeknownst to him, thought I had been called into work for some mysterious reason. I had been caught in flagrante delicto, so to speak.

"I could suspend you without pay, Stef," he said solemnly.

"But you're not going to do that?" Barbie leaned forward and flashed him a toothy smile.

I could see him blush as he glanced from her pearly whites down to her giant boobs.

His pudgy face turned bright red as he swallowed. "No," he said, with considerable difficulty. "I'm going to let it slide."

My mother gave him a big "You're my hero" sigh.

With more considerable difficulty, Warthog turned away from Barbie and settled his beady little eyes back on me. "But no more, okay, Stef?"

All I could do was nod my head and mutter an "I'm sorry."

"You don't mind if I talk to Steffie for a few minutes, do you?" Barbie asked.

Please mind, please mind, I willed.

"Of course not," he said, practically beaming.

"Thank you so much, Mr. Warzog," she said sweetly.

Then she grabbed my arm and yanked me out of his office and through the back door, to where the deliveries are made. She stopped and turned to face me. Her eyes were bulging and her neck was beginning to blotch. Even so, she still looked hot. "Are you crazy? You were in the water!" she shouted. "And you lied to me!"

"Maybe you should call your friend Emily Mills and tell her about it. She might be able to give you some advice. After all, she's got a century of experience under her belt," I snapped. I couldn't stop myself.

"So that's what this is about. You're punishing me."

"Not everything is about you, Barbie."

"I beg your pardon?" She reeled backward dramatically, as if my words had cut her to her very soul.

I winced as I recognized the superangry tone in my mother's voice. I couldn't even imagine what this whole thing was going to cost me. Unfortunately, even though I was practically a legal adult, Barbie still wielded enough power over me to make my life a living hell. Although she couldn't really pull off normal punishments like restrictions (because she was never home herself and therefore unable to enforce them) or taking away my car keys (for obvious reasons), she fought dirty. For instance, if I was sleeping, one of my favorite possessions would just go AWOL. She would stop at nothing. My favorite DVDs, my favorite articles of clothing. One time last year, I'd waked up to find that the TV was gone. Eventually, the items would return, but in the case of the TV, it was gone for an entire week. Punishments in the Rogers household were nothing if not cruel and unusual.

"Did you forget who you're talking to?" Barbie said through clenched teeth. "Do I need to remind you who puts the roof over your head?"

In the past, I might have answered these rhetorical questions with something like: "Did I ask to be born?" But I no longer felt the need to remind her of such a primary fact.

So instead I said, "I'm your daughter. Yet you continue to make choices that have a negative effect on me and my life. Like making me move every time you get your heart broken."

I'd found in previous arguments that my mother had no idea when she was being hit smack in the face with psychobabble. She thought I was a lot smarter than I actually was. If I kept calm and talked about choices and negative effects, she just assumed I knew what I was talking about.

Her eyes narrowed and she said, "No more swimming lessons, got it? I don't want you near the pool again." She put her hands over her heart. "The thought of it is giving me palpitations."

But unlike her, I wasn't in the mood for promises that I had no intention of keeping (although the irrational fear thing was still working for me).

"I have to go," I said, and boldly walked away.

When I got home after work, I was shocked to see the TV still perched on the table across from the couch. In fact, despite my certainty that something would be gone, everything was still in its place. Weird, very weird. Not to mention unnerving. But even my mother's weirdness couldn't affect my surprisingly lightening mood. I had to get over to Alice's to watch my hunky lifeguard-with-a-girlfriend mow the yard.

I put on a yellow wannabe Tommy Hilfiger sundress and then took it off because I thought it looked too obvious, like I was still harboring the idea that he might like me-like me. I finally settled on a "no mistaking it, we're just friends" outfit consisting of a clean white American Eagle tank top from two years ago, black shorts from the Gap (last year's summer line), and my duct-taped flip-flops.

When I got to Alice's, we sat on her back porch in one-hundred-degree first-day-of-August heat until we heard a loud whirring sound. We walked around front just as Keith came rolling in on a gigantic monster truck of a lawn mower. He was wearing a navy blue baseball hat with VARSITY CLUB written on it and these camouflage-print cutoff shorts that were ragged at the knees. His black T-shirt was already sticking to him, and he gave us a friendly wave as he started mowing.

"So what do I do?" I asked Alice.

She took out a handkerchief from a striped capri pants pocket and wiped at her cleavage. "What do you mean?"

"Am I supposed to go talk to him?"

"It's going to be hard to have a conversation while the lawn mower is going. Why don't you wait until he's done and then ask him inside for some iced tea?"

It sounded easy enough. I could certainly handle that without breaking into a dripping sweat, right?

I followed Alice back inside and into the kitchen, where she was preparing one of my favorites: pot roast with mashed potatoes and gravy. This may have seemed like an odd meal to make when it was a million degrees outside and two million degrees inside, but Alice had never let the temperature interfere with her cooking. She said it was all a matter of what you were used to, and for the past forty years she had made sure there was a hot meal on her table every night.

My mind flashed forward to six months from now. Barbie and Ludwig were on the skids and the map of Maryland was out again and Barbie's finger was about to land somewhere far away from Jones Island, and then Alice was helping me pack before we said our final goodbyes.

I shook my head and tried to rid myself of such

fatalistic thoughts. I did have a doomed relationship to foster, after all.

After I helped Alice finish peeling the potatoes, I went into the living room and paced around, pausing every now and then to glance out the window to check on Keith's progress.

"Alice," I said when he was almost finished. "What if he doesn't stop the mower? What if he just drives off without stopping to talk to me?"

"Steffie," she yelled out from the kitchen, "you're the reason why he's here. He's not going to leave without seeing you."

"I thought you said he was just trying to be nice," I shouted back to her.

"Well, he might have been in the beginning." She walked into the living room. "But I think all the attention he's been giving you is more than just him being nice."

My toes were tingling at the mere mention of him wanting more. "What about Mora?"

"I wouldn't worry about her. From what happened today, it's obvious Mora's a replica of her mother. And Keith," she said, nodding out the window as Keith drove past on his mower, "is too nice and smart to end up with a woman like that."

Alice had been furious when I told her about the whole Mora-trying-to-get-me-fired thing. So furious, in fact, that I almost wished I hadn't told her. She'd asked me to spend the evening at her house and make a Mora voodoo doll out of a pincushion, which was both funny and scary at the same time (because I really, really wanted to do it).

She put her arm around me and gave me a good squeeze. "He's probably going through a hot sex phase. God knows I've been there!"

I elbowed Alice in the ribs. "Ew! Thanks for the visual!"

She started laughing so hard she went into another coughing fit.

I stepped away from the window, worried that Keith had seen me staring at him and Alice guffawing like a hyena. "It's weird that he's over here mowing your yard, isn't it? I mean, it's so nice of him." I said this partially to convince myself that Keith's mowing Alice's yard was largely due to the fact that he found me oh-so-irresistible.

Alice sat down on the sofa and put her feet up on the ottoman. "Not really." (She completely missed the cue where she was supposed to jump in and tell me again how much he secretly liked me!) "Keith's just a good person, and that's what good people do."

Suddenly, I heard the lawn mower's engine cut out. I stepped back to the window just in time to see Keith pick up his shirt and use it to wipe the sweat from his brow.

"That was fast." I gulped as I stared at his incredibly toned torso.

"Go on, Stef," Alice said, nodding toward outside. "Now's your chance."

As I stepped outside, I felt a flutter of nerves, the same feeling I had in fifth grade when I had to recite the line "Papa, the Wells Fargo wagon is a-comin'!" in a (very lame) school performance of *The Music Man*.

"Hey." Keith greeted me with his signature gasp-inducing smile.

I took a deep breath. "Do you want something to drink?" I asked.

"Thanks, but I have some water." He hopped off the mower and took a swig from the bottle that he had kept in his messenger bag.

I nervously glanced toward the house as my mind went blank. What was I supposed to say next? "Thanks for mowing," I said mechanically as I squashed a mosquito on my arm.

Suave. Especially the part when I flicked the dead mosquito away and rubbed the blood off with my thumb.

"No problem," he said. "Tell Alice I'm happy to help out whenever."

I wrung my hands together nervously. "Herbert Lewis usually does it." He was the freckly-faced seventh grader who lived in the apartment below mine. "He's visiting his dad in Virginia. Do you know Herbert?" I asked.

"Um—I don't think so." Keith took off his hat and

shook his head a bit. Then something amazing happened. A little bead of his sweat landed on my shoulder!

Quite honestly, I lost every shred of composure I had maintained up until that moment. I could feel that my leg was bobbing up and down just like Barbie's had been earlier that day, and I began tugging at the strap of my tank top that was closest to where his sweat had landed, in a vain effort to touch his fluids. My end of the conversation was totally shot.

There was a moment of silence as Keith glanced around Alice's yard, as if admiring his handiwork. He also seemed unaware of the fact that I wanted to tackle him and roll around in his handiwork. "So were you going to level this whole thing with a push mower?"

I nodded.

"Wow," he said, impressed. "It's got to be, like, what? At least two acres, right?"

"I guess," I said. Two acres. Two hundred acres. *Keith McKnight's sweat was on my body!*

"Not too many places around here have this much property."

"That's because the houses are so big."

"True." His beautiful eyes darted across the creek to his house. He shook his head. "Big and awful."

"I like your house, Keith." For some reason, I took a step toward him. "It's very . . . palacelike."

Ick.

"Thanks," Keith said, and smirked. "I shouldn't complain, though. At least it's big enough for me to not have to deal with anyone that much."

"I wouldn't know what that's like," I said. "My mom and I pretty much live on top of each other. I liked our apartment before this one a lot better. The dining area was separate from the living room." As I stared into Keith's eyes, I could feel a smile creeping across my face that was not even the slightest bit secret.

"Where was that?" he asked.

"In Hagerstown."

"Hagerstown?"

"It's on the other side of the state, near West Virginia."

"I know exactly where it is," he said. "I go to school in Frostburg, so we drive through Hagerstown all the time. What made you guys decide to move here?"

It felt as though something was lodged in my throat. Now we were getting into uncharted territory. The last thing I wanted to do was come across as some sort of crazy sap, which I was, but he didn't need to know that *now*, did he? And how could I explain our constant moves without giving away too much information?

"Stef?" Alice peeked her head out and rescued me as if on cue. "Could you help me with something?"

"I'll be right back." I hurried back inside like a boxer retreating to his corner.

"How's it going?" Alice whispered. She handed me a glass of ice water.

"Exhausting," I replied before gulping it down (even though I knew she had intended it for Keith). "Who would think that making conversation with a guy would be so hard?" I said when I was finished.

"It's not just a guy, though," Alice said with a lilt in her voice. "It's Keith."

I wasn't sure if I was glistening from the heat outside or what, but I was feeling rather dewy all of sudden. "I know. But Barbie makes it look so easy."

"When it comes to flirting, your mother's in a league of her own," Alice agreed. "But she has years of experience. You just need some more practice." She paused for a minute and then asked, "Do you feel up to inviting him for dinner?"

I hesitated, and Alice said, "We'll never eat all that food by ourselves. And besides, the pickles I made the other day are ready."

Alice was right. Keith had mowed her yard. As nerve-wracking as I found the whole concept of his staying for dinner, the least I could do was reward him with some pickles.

I took another deep breath, handed Alice back the empty glass, and returned to the ring. Keith was leaning against his lawn mower with his head back and arms crossed, soaking up the last rays of sunshine.

"Would you like to stay for dinner?" I blurted out.

He opened his eyes and stood up straight. "I'm sorry, I can't. I'm having dinner with my dad. But thanks anyway."

"Sure," I replied, secretly relieved. Due to the sudden itchiness of my chest, I was pretty certain I was breaking out in hives.

He looked at me and smiled as we endured an awkward silence. Dinner with his dad or not, he was obviously in no rush. His seeming reluctance to leave was confusing. Not that I was anxious for him to go, but why was he gazing at me like that? Oh God, was there something hanging out of my nose?

"We should schedule another lesson," he said finally. "How about tomorrow night?"

"Warthog . . . I mean, Mr. Warzog didn't talk to you?" I asked.

"About what?"

"He found out about me being at the pool when it was closed." Considering that Keith's father was one of the club's best golfers, I wasn't really surprised that Warthog had not even bothered to mention this to Keith. "He told me it was against club rules."

"What?" Keith said tersely. He was visibly surprised. "When did he tell you that?"

"This morning."

He swiped back his hair as his eyes narrowed. "How did he even know you were there?"

I was tempted to accuse Mora, but I could hear my elementary school teacher's voice in my ear reminding me that no one liked a tattletale. "I guess somebody complained," I said graciously.

"Mora." He shook his head in seeming disgust.

I shrugged. "He didn't say."

The muscles in his jaw tightened. "I hate all this bullcrap. I mean, why the hell do they care if you're at the pool when it's not open? You *work* there."

I shrugged again.

"Not to mention that you're around that pool all the time. And you almost drowned in it. People should mind their own damn business."

I couldn't believe how irate he was getting, and it was all because of . . . me.

"All right," he said resolutely. "We'll just move our lessons to the bay."

My heart dropped. We were once again way off script. How could I tell him that there was no way in hell I was going into that bay? It was one thing to be at the pool when there was at least the slightest sense that "the man" was watching over us all the time. But the *bay*? We were just asking for something unexpectedly romantic to happen. This was not an option. I would just have to let him down easy and tell him under no circumstances could I allow myself to be vulnerable to the likes of love lunacy, or the jellyfish, crabs, and other squirmy, smelly creatures that were lurking in the bay.

"How about Friday night?" he asked. "I can meet you at Crab Beach after I get off work around seven."

I looked into his deep brown eyes and smiled in spite of myself. "Sounds good," I said.

10

On Friday morning, I went to work and soon found out that life as I knew it was no more. I was no longer invisible.

How did I know this?

Because of the Cola Catastrophe.

Shortly after lunch, I headed to the pool for the daily sanitization of the bathrooms. As I made my way through the crowd of bathing beauties, I saw Mora lying on a lounge chair in her thong bikini (so overkill) and sipping a diet soda (food and drinks were prohibited in the pool area—but because she was *the* Mora Cooper, she could have eaten a lobster on the sundeck and nobody would have cared). Our eyes locked and she sneered at me in a way that made it extremely clear she was not happy to see me. I felt a little chill prick my skin, an almost extrasensory hint of disaster. But I decided to ignore her and the chill. And just to prove that

I wasn't intimidated by her god-awful stare, I walked right past her.

And then it happened. Her almost empty can of soda came spiraling through the air, bouncing off me and landing beside my foot, where the remainder of her drink pooled around my white plastic shoes.

"Oops," Mora said coolly, looking me directly in the eye. Instead of apologizing, she motioned toward the cement with her red-lacquered toe and said, "*Maid!* Can you clean that up? I don't want it to get all buggy."

All of Mora's friends—Liv Reynolds, yearbook editor and fourth cousin of Ralph Lauren; Suzanne Perling, head of the prom committee and a senator's daughter; and Georgie Sweetwater, state beauty queen and total airhead—started snickering. I thought about what Alice would have done had this been her—probably something along the lines of making Mora lick the soda off the sole of her shoe (Suzanne too, because her father was a Republican). This made me determined to teach Mora a lesson. I wiped my sticky hands on my uniform, took a step toward her, reached inside my pocket, and then . . .

I pulled out a rag, bent down, and wiped up the soda.

"Oh, c'mon, Steffie!" Alice exclaimed when I told her what had happened. We were in the laundry room folding thick white towels and tablecloths. "You call that a comeback? Why didn't you throw down with that skank?"

I laughed so hard that I knocked my pile of clean washcloths onto the floor. I loved it when Alice talked all gangsta. "What good would that have done?"

Alice opened up a tablecloth and shook it free of lint. "It would've made you feel better, for one."

"It was awful," I confided. "Now I know how Barbie felt when she got nailed with merlot." Right before we'd moved last year, Barbie had been working as a waitress at this above-average Italian restaurant. One day, a woman she had never met walked right up to her and tossed a glass of red wine in her face.

"Let me guess," Alice said. "She was a jealous wife."

I picked up the washcloths and threw them back in the dirty pile. "Yep."

"This isn't the same thing. Mora is not married to Keith. And you haven't done anything wrong. Mora is just being crazy. That's all." Alice shook her head. "Maybe you should talk to Mr. Warzog. Let him know what happened."

"No," I said. "I'd rather forget about it."

"Well," Alice said finally, "there is a bright side to all this. I'm obviously not the only one who thinks that Keith is interested in you."

And that changed *everything*.

Unlike the evening of his party, I felt no inclination to stay home and watch TV that night. Come hell or high water, I was going to Crab Beach. When I got home from work, I pulled out all the stops, like blow-drying my hair with Barbie's big round brush and flicking on some CoverGirl waterproof mascara and lipgloss. And then just so I wouldn't be that obvious, I put on my standard beachwear: peach-colored T-shirt, secondhand J.Crew drawstring jean shorts, and Barbie's prized slightly platform flip-flops.

It was dusk when I arrived, and a shirtless Keith was sitting on Crab Beach's thin strip of sand, waiting for me. Like most "beaches" on the Chesapeake, Crab Beach was just a grassy, reedy area. But because Keith was gracing this place with his glowing presence, it felt as though we were on the shores of Belize, peering out at the infinite topaz ocean.

"Hey." Keith stood up and blocked the sun like an eclipse. "How are you?"

"Good." My hands were trembling.

Keith was quiet for a second and I heard the water gently lapping up against the marsh's edge. He seemed uncomfortable, as if he was about to disappoint me or something.

"I heard what happened today at the pool," he said, and looked down at his feet.

I didn't answer.

He made a design in the sand with his heel. "I'm really sorry, Steffie."

I calculated how many steps I'd have to take to be close enough to kiss him. Five. "Why are you apologizing? It's not your fault. Besides, I'm sure it was an, uh, accident."

"You're being nice," he said. Suddenly he looked me in the eye and his awkwardness vanished. "Mora and I have a complicated relationship. We've been working through some . . . things lately, and I feel bad that she took it out on you."

The news that Keith and Mora were having problems sent a tremor of elation straight through me. "That's too bad," I managed to say.

He walked toward me a little bit. Four steps left. "We're both kind of at a crossroads, trying to figure out if this . . . us . . . is, well, worth it."

"How long have you guys been together?" I asked, even though I already knew the answer to that question, as did everyone else within a ten-mile radius.

Keith did an about-face and headed toward the water. Eight, nine, ten. "We've been friends for a long time and hooked up last summer. We broke up when I went back to school."

I decided to follow him, but stood a safe distance away. "I didn't know you broke up."

He nodded. "Yeah. I mean, not to get too personal or anything, but I was studying philosophy at school and it just gave me a different perspective on Jones Island and life in general. I felt like I really didn't have that much in common with the kids around here anymore. They all seemed so . . . shallow. There was no depth to them at all."

I couldn't believe this. Keith was wearing his heart on his proverbial sleeve, and there was no one around to appreciate it but me.

"So when I came back this summer, I really didn't have any intention of hooking up with Mora again. But our parents are good friends, and Mora and I kept getting thrown together. She seemed like she had really grown up a lot in the past year. The way she's been acting recently, though . . . Well, I'm beginning to wonder."

I suddenly realized he was staring right at me. I wanted to say something profound and eloquent, as if I was in Keith's philosophy class, but I was so afraid to screw it up. I knew if I kept looking at him I would, so I turned my attention to the water and inhaled the salty air. "No one's ever what we expect them to be."

Whoa. Where had that come from?

I glanced back at Keith, and his eyes were glimmering.

Who cared? He'd obviously liked it.

"That's true," he said, grinning. "Anyway, I didn't mean to drag you into all this."

"It's okay." I smiled.

"Thanks for being so understanding." He stretched his arms over his head and then put his hands on his hips. "All right, ready to go swimming?"

I was so ready that I shed my clothes in less than

twenty seconds. Meanwhile, Keith pulled out a long piece of rope from his duffel bag and untied it.

"You're not nervous, are you?" he asked.

I shook my head. It was really weird, but I wasn't nervous at all.

"Good," he said. "There's not much of a current, but I don't want to take any chances." He looped one side of the rope around my waist before tying the other side around his own.

Keith tucked a kickboard under his arm and we walked side by side across the hard pebble-filled sand and into the warm, dark water, wading in until it was up to our waists. I was remarkably cool and collected. At least, I was until I saw the giant white fleshy creature speeding toward me with fangs bared.

"Jellyfish!" I screamed, practically hopping into Keith's arms.

He plucked the white glob out of the water and held it up. "Paper." He smirked. "This water can get kind of gross this time of year. But the good news is there's no jellyfish yet."

"Great," I said weakly. Suddenly I realized that Keith still had his arm around me. He seemed to realize it at the same time, because we both took a step backward and cleared our throats.

"Here you go," he said, handing me the kickboard. "Just start kicking," he said. "I'll walk alongside you."

I glanced out across the bay. The masts of several

sailboats dotted the horizon, bobbing lazily in the dusk. It was a clear night, and I could see the skyline of Annapolis in the distance as lights began to fill the shoreline. It was an altogether peaceful scene. It did not look like the bay my mother had described: a seemingly tamed beast that was capable of turning ferocious in an instant. It was just another thing that we saw completely differently.

"Go on," Keith said, encouraging me.

You can do this, I reassured myself. I would not be one of those silly squeamish girls who let their fears hold them back. And with that final thought, I leaned over the board and began to kick. After a while, I forgot about the crabs and the jellyfish. (They hadn't arrived *yet*. What did that mean? Were they on their way?) Finally, Keith took my board away and tossed it back onto the beach.

"I want you to move your hands like this." He showed me the stroke once again. As he reached forward and then back, the muscles in his arms popped to the surface. "Got it?"

I nodded and dropped back into the water. He lifted me up, and I began to kick and move my arms. "Good," he said. He moved his hands out from underneath me and I immediately began to sink.

"Are you okay?" he asked, lifting me back up.

"Fine," I said, pushing the hair out of my eyes.

"Concentrate," I heard him say.

And then a thought popped into my head. He was close enough to kiss me.

Suddenly, I was completely underwater and Keith's strong arms were pulling me to the surface.

I coughed up the water I had inhaled, but fortunately, there was no barf involved. It was gross nonetheless. The bay is pretty much grody salt water mixed with motor oil (i.e., not much better than the pee water in the pool).

"Let's take a break," Keith said, hastily removing his hands from my waist.

As I followed him back to the shore, I couldn't help noticing that he seemed disappointed, like a teacher whose star student had just flunked.

"I'm sorry," I said softly after he had untied us.

"Don't worry," he said, grabbing his towel and plopping down on the sand. "You'll get it."

He handed me my purple beach towel, and his thumb grazed mine. I tied the towel around my waist before sitting down next to him. And there we were. Two people sitting side by side. In kissing proximity.

"I saw your mom last night," he announced out of the blue.

My eyelids started twitching. "Barbie?"

He nodded. "After I had dinner with my dad, I went to a party on the beach. There were a lot of people from the club there."

I imagined my mom dancing in her bra and underpants, or something else that would ruin my life forever. My eyelids twitched faster.

"It's the first time I ever talked to her," he said. "She seems nice."

I knew that I should have accepted this as the compliment it was intended to be and moved on. But instead I blurted out, "She's crazy."

So much for eloquent and profound.

He raised his eyebrows. I thought I could see the hint of a smile.

"I mean, not certifiably insane but, well, she's very different from me."

"How so?"

Wrap it up, I cautioned myself. "She has affairs with married men." *Yep, that ought to do it.*

"Married men?" he repeated incredulously.

I picked up a stray twig and began playing with it absentmindedly. "That's why we move so often. Every time a relationship breaks up, she wants to start fresh. At least, that's how she justifies it."

Keith kept his gaze on me. "How often have you moved?"

"Fourteen times."

His eyes widened in surprise. "Wow, so every year you go to a different school?"

"Almost. This is the first time I can remember that

I'm actually going to be attending the same school two years in a row."

Keith stretched his legs out and leaned back on his arms. "That's got to be tough. My mom and I moved to D.C. when my parents separated and I was in middle school. I still remember how weird it was to walk into the cafeteria and see all these people hanging out and talking to each other and realize that I didn't know a single person. There wasn't one familiar face."

"Story of my life," I said, breaking the twig in half.

"Have you thought about where you want to go to college?"

"In state, that's for sure." I told him about the small but growing tuition fund that my mom and I had set up. I put in seventy-five percent of my Tippecanoe earnings and she matched it, even if it meant she had to work an extra shift.

"That's nice that your mom's helping you."

This comment irked me. I rarely thought of Barbie as being helpful. "Yeah, but what's not so nice is that she's threatened to walk with my money if I don't go to college. She told me she would just use it to take herself on a really nice long vacation—sans yours truly."

He chuckled. This irked me too. Barbie's dysfunction was rarely funny.

"So you think that's amusing?" I asked.

Keith took his foot and tapped it against mine. Magically, I wasn't irked anymore. "I don't mean to laugh.

Really, Stef, it just sounds like she wants to make sure you have a better life than she's had."

I already knew this, of course. And now that I thought more about it, it was sweet that he had made my kooky mother's threats about absconding with my hard-earned money sound sane.

"Have you thought about what you might want to study?" The sun was dropping every minute, but it was still warm. Keith's swim trunks were almost dry.

"Psychology. I feel like I've been my mom's therapist for years."

Keith let out another laugh. This time I was happy I was the cause of it. "No kidding."

"Yeah, it would be nice to actually get paid for my work. And to have patients who actually listen to my advice."

His eyebrows rose again. Adorable. "Your mom doesn't listen to you?"

"Unfortunately, no," I said, shaking my head. "If she did, our life would be a lot different."

"How so?"

"Well, for one, she wouldn't be working as a cocktail waitress. She could've gotten about ten degrees with all the time she's wasted on dead-end relationships."

He grinned. "You seem like you've got it together, Stef. I know your life can't be easy, working and going to school like you do. But I think it's cool. You're like Alice in that way. You don't need money to be happy."

He glanced out at the bay. "Maybe you can give me pointers. Up until now, I've only had to pay for all the incidental stuff at school, like books and stuff, and my dad has paid for everything else. But as he informed me a couple weeks ago, nothing comes for free."

I must've looked confused, because he said, "He's willing to pay as long as I study law or medicine." All of a sudden he cupped his hands together and opened them. He had caught a lightning bug. How cute/gross! "The problem is, I don't want to be a lawyer or a doctor. I want to be an entomologist."

The fact that he was holding a bug should've been a clue, but I had no idea what he was talking about.

"I want to study bugs," he added.

A nonchalant *How interesting* would've been an appropriate response. Instead, I said, "I love bugs!" Me. The one who screamed whenever a bee flew near, the one who had never met a spider she hadn't squashed.

"You do?"

I looked into those glimmering eyes and nodded.

He furrowed his brow. "You're an unusual girl."

"What exactly do entomologists do?" I was trying hard to act as though I was really interested, like, *Hmmm, maybe I'll forget about this psych stuff and become an entomologist instead!*

"There are different kinds. There's forensic entomologists, the guys you see on TV who can determine when a person died by the bugs on the corpse."

Or maybe I wouldn't.

"But most entomologists study insects that are beneficial or harmful to humans," Keith explained. "For instance, there's a study going on right now with this form of beetles. They can eat battery acid and turn it into a substance that is harmless. Think of how great it would be if we could cultivate bugs that could eat some of the products that are just overflowing in our landfills."

I absolutely loved the fact that he was a smartie. "That would be great," I said. "So what are you going to do?"

"Change my major. I'll figure out a way to pay for it myself."

I also absolutely loved the fact that Keith felt okay about being poor. Well, maybe not poor, but poorer. It leveled the playing field a bit.

"Come here." He stood up and offered me his hand. "I want to show you something."

He pulled me to my feet and led me through the beat-down grass and up a craggy path lined with reeds. We walked in silence, surrounded by the almost deafening hum of crickets. We got to the top of the bluff and stopped on a precipice overlooking the bay. "My mom used to take me here as a kid," he said.

"It's beautiful," I said.

"There's a swim meet tomorrow night in Easton." He hesitated as the smile faded from his mouth. "Watching the pros might help you pick up the strokes much easier. If you want to go, I could take you."

Did I want to go to a swim meet with him? Did birds fly? Did hearts beat? Did I love bugs?

Then I remembered something. An obligation that I couldn't get out of. And a disease that I just couldn't afford to catch.

"I can't," I said. "It's bingo night."

Keith didn't say another word. And neither did I. We just stood there, watching our moonlit reflections wiggle in the current of cloudy water.

11

Steffie Rogers's most shocking moments (from least to most):

1) When I thought my bra size had increased. (Turns out Barbie had thrown my bras in the dryer by mistake.)
2) When I passed chemistry.
3) When Keith offered me free swimming lessons.
4) When I found out that after years of hating broccoli—I actually liked it.
5) When my mother said that a married man had asked her out and she had turned him down.
6) When I ate what I thought was a piece of chicken and it turned out to be frog legs. Disgusting!
7) When I turned down an opportunity to attend a swim meet with the man of *my* dreams to play bingo.

Obviously, I was not easily shocked. But turning down a date (official or not) with Keith to play bingo was a topper.

Not that I didn't enjoy the bingo nights. I did. In fact, they were usually the highlight of my life. But that was just the point. I went nearly every other week. How often did I have an opportunity to go to a swim meet? But it was too late for regrets. I had to focus on the positive. Like the fact that even though I was totally into Keith, I had not thrown my friends over just because I had gotten a better offer. (Like Barbie would've done.) I was not a fair-weather friend. Nosiree. And I was fairly certain Alice would appreciate my sacrifice.

"What!" Alice's friend Doris said as we finished our first round of food at the China Buffet. "You passed up a date for a night of bingo and Chinese food with a bunch of old ladies?"

I glanced at Alice for support. "Maybe you should give her some of your Xanax, Dor," she said.

I rolled my eyes. "It wasn't a date. It was a swim meet. Besides, he has a girlfriend."

"Mora," Doris said, as if the mere word was distasteful. She finished chewing a mouthful of fried rice before saying, "Don't get me started on her."

"Isabella said they've been having problems for a long time," Alice's other friend, Thelma, added.

"Isabella, Isabella, Isabella," Doris said. "Can we

have one conversation without bringing up the Coopers' maid?"

Alice and I exchanged a glance. Doris and Thelma were the odd couple of the island. Although they'd been best friends since the first grade, they were opposites in every way. Doris was thin; Thelma was fat. Doris was blond; Thelma wore a giant red wig. Doris was loud; Thelma was quiet. And of course, Doris was upper-middle-class and Thelma was filthy, stinking rich.

"Girls," Alice said loudly, breaking up the fight before things got ugly. "We should finish up and go."

"Is that all you're eating?" Doris looked at Alice's plate.

But the question was rhetorical. We knew there was absolutely no chance that Alice (or any of us, for that matter) wouldn't go back for seconds, thirds, and fourths. Because that was what we did. We'd get tiny portions and then go back for "a little bit more." And then a little bit more. And then just another bite (after all, we might as well get our money's worth). There was a lot of talk about how we weren't going to eat lunch the next day, and sometimes we'd even talk about how we weren't going to eat lunch *or* dinner. And then we'd go back and get dessert.

"I'm just not that hungry," Alice replied.

We all sat there, too stunned to reply. Doris broke our silence. "You'd think you were the one in love, instead of Steffie."

My ears perked up. How did we get back on that subject? I looked at Alice for help, but she was studying her noodles as if they had suddenly turned into a plate of worms.

"I think they put too much pepper in here," Alice said, horrified.

"Then go get another plate," I suggested.

Alice shook her head, just like I knew she would. Alice *hated* to waste food. One thing I learned from sharing so many meals with Alice was that I needed to finish whatever was on my plate. She wouldn't actually force-feed me, but if I didn't gobble everything up, she'd just look so upset that I'd will myself to finish. It was kind of confusing because my mother encouraged me to do just the opposite. *"It's a great way to manage your weight,"* Barbie had once said. *"Don't deprive yourself of anything, just take two bites and throw the rest out."*

"I just can't get over the fact that our little Steffie is in love with Mora's boyfriend." Doris shook her head and chomped down on a piece of broccoli. A tiny piece of it got caught in her dentures. "My, my, my."

"I'm not in love with anyone's boyfriend." I jabbed at my egg roll with my fork.

"I can't eat this," Alice said as she began to cough. She tapped her chest and said, "It's so peppery, I can barely breathe."

"Then go get something else," I repeated, mildly annoyed. I mean, I knew Alice hated to waste food and all, but hello? Didn't she notice that I was getting the third degree? I could have used some assistance.

"I never understood what Keith saw in Mora in the first place," Doris said. She spent a lot of time at Tippecanoe playing Yahtzee and gossiping with a group of widows Alice called the Gold Rush Girls (because they were around at the time of the gold rush—ha!).

"No one did," Thelma added as she sipped on some wonton soup.

"Why did they put all that pepper in there?" Alice groaned. "They ruined it!"

Doris ignored Alice. "I say: Good for you!" she exclaimed.

Thelma applauded.

"For the last time," I said. "It was a swim meet. Not an invitation to the prom."

Everyone just stared at me. Everyone but Alice, who was still looking at her plate.

"If he asks me again, I'll go." I took another bite of lo mein.

"*If* he asks again," Thelma said.

"What do you mean, *if he asks?*" I choked on a noodle.

"Well, you did turn him down," Doris said. "And you know men. Their egos are—"

"Fragile," Thelma interrupted.

I got a sinking feeling in the pit of my stomach. Maybe these wacky old broads were right. Maybe Keith would never ask me out again. Ever. "What do you think, Alice?" I asked. "Do you think he'll ask me out again?"

But Alice wasn't paying attention to me. She was fiddling with her chopsticks, looking as if she might cry.

"Are you all right?" I asked.

"I'm sorry, girls," she mumbled. "But I think I'm going to go home."

"But we haven't even played bingo yet!" I said.

"I know, but I . . ." She stopped and looked at me. "I'm just feeling a little tired tonight."

"But Alice, it's bingo night," I whined.

"You don't have to go home by yourself," Doris said. "We can all go. We don't have to play bingo."

I had turned down an opportunity to hang out with Keith for *this*?

"No," Alice insisted. "Please stay and have fun. I'll be perfectly fine." Then she turned to Thelma and said, "Would you mind driving Steffie home?"

"Maybe some more iced tea would perk you up," I suggested helpfully to Alice.

She shot me a weak smile as she rose from the table. "Win a round for me tonight, okay? I'll see you tomorrow at work."

As Alice walked out, I put down my fork, suffering from a sudden sense of déjà vu.

"What was that all about?" I asked Thelma.

Thelma just shrugged. "That's Alice for you."

But that wasn't Alice. At least, not the Alice I knew. I was going through kind of a hard time here. I needed her. Why would she just up and leave because she was feeling tired? And suddenly I realized where all that déjà vu was coming from. This was something Barbie would have done.

"Well," Doris said in a forced cheery voice. "Should we check out the desserts before we go?" But even though they had some really good-looking trifle desserts (I loved vanilla pudding and I loved yellow cake—especially when they were mixed together), I had only one serving.

After dinner, the three of us piled into Thelma's fancy schmancy black Lincoln sedan and drove to the bingo hall. It definitely was not as good as being with Keith, but as I had mentioned, I liked bingo. Each player donated one dollar to the winner's till, and there were always at least a hundred people, so this was serious business. I'd had amazing luck and had won five games out of the twenty we'd played.

The three of us staked out a spot as the ladies talked about Roy Gilroy, the bingo director. A small man with a walrus mustache, Roy was the Keith McKnight of the Alice generation. Roy took his seat on a director's chair and began pulling letters out of the big black box in front of him. When Alice, Doris, Thelma, or I won, it was a big deal, but if we lost, it was a *really big* sucktastic deal. And wouldn't you know it, we lost. Every single one of us.

Unfortunately for me, my night was about to get worse. Much worse.

Because when I walked into my apartment, I was welcomed home by the sight of my mother making out with none other than Ludwig van Beethoven.

12

She was standing in the main entrance, hungrily kissing him as if his lips were covered in Cheesy Nacho Hamburger Helper. I knew I should've just been thankful that they both had their clothes on. Unfortunately for them, however, I wasn't feeling grateful.

"Steffie!" Barbie untangled herself and tucked her almost sheer black blouse into her snug jeans. "You're back early!"

Ludwig was tall and attractive, with blue eyes and thick black hair peppered with gray. He kept his cool, nodding as I gave him the once-over. "You must be Steffie," he said, sticking out his hand.

I thought about dissing him and shoving my hand in my pocket, but unfortunately, I thought about it after I had already shaken his. I was relieved to discover that he had a nice firm handshake, not clammy or sweaty.

"I'm Tom," he said, stopping short of giving his last name.

"Hi," I said tersely.

He let go of my hand quickly. "I should get going."

"I'll walk you out," my mom said while escorting him to his car.

I felt my face go hot. Sure, there had to be a first time for everything, but did I really have to meet one of my mother's boyfriends that night? I was having a hard enough time with my own love lunacy problems.

"So how was bingo?" my mother asked, reappearing a few minutes later with her blouse untucked once again.

It was as clear as Scotch tape that Barbie was an optimist. Case in point: thinking that there was a chance of my *not* mentioning that I had just interrupted a giant smooching session was damn near crazy optimistic.

"It sucked," I replied.

"Oh no!" Barbie was trying to act disappointed, but it was such a big crock. My mom hated my bingo nights. At first she'd thought it was kind of funny that I was playing bingo at the senior center, but then when I started really getting into it, she began to get annoyed. On bingo nights, she'd started offering to take me to the movies or out to dinner at the Red Lobster (I had a thing for their hush puppies) just so I'd cancel. But it hadn't worked because, as I'd explained to her, I needed to make my own friends. She'd replied that she wanted me to make my own friends too, which was why she didn't like to see me hanging out with a bunch of "grandmas."

"The whole apartment reeks of Polo Sport," I announced. Barbie started tidying up the pillows on the couch and ignored me. So I got right in her face. "I hope he didn't hurry off on my account. Was his wife expecting him home? Did he need to go back and tuck his kids into bed?"

"Don't start, Steffie," she said quietly.

Just go to bed, I commanded myself. After all, did I really want to get into a big fight with her tonight? "In the future," I said, "I'd appreciate it if you didn't bring your men around here."

"My *men?*" Barbie said.

Normally I would've had enough common sense to abort. But again, I was in a terrible mood. Maybe a big blowout fight was just what I needed.

"It makes me sick to think about them, never mind meet them," I said through gritted teeth.

My mother glared at me and crossed her arms. "Well, I would think you, of all people, would be willing to cut me some slack. Especially considering your present situation."

I stopped still. "What present situation?"

"Oh, please, Steffie. Everyone at the club knows you have the hots for Mora Cooper's boyfriend."

"That's ridiculous!" I forced a laugh (which came out sounding like a crazy cackle).

Barbie stared me down. "Then why did Mora throw a drink at you?"

I was speechless. How had this confrontation ended up being about me and my love life? "Mora happened to spill her drink while I was there. I cleaned it up. It's what I'm hired to do. End of subject."

"You're not interested in Keith McKnight?" she asked, peering at me suspiciously.

At times like these, I really wished I was a better liar. I just stood there, trying to shake my head.

My mother exhaled long and slow. "All these years, when you kept asking me why I dated married men and I kept telling you that you can't control who you love . . ."

"This isn't like that," I said quickly.

"Of course not. Because now it's happening to you."

"I don't have to put up with this," I said. And then, just to make it crystal clear, I spun around and headed for the door. "I'm leaving."

"Don't you dare walk out on me, young lady!" Barbie yelled.

I slammed the door behind me and jumped on my bike. I pedaled to Alice's house as fast as I could, tears stinging my eyes block after block. How could my mother act as if she had done nothing wrong? How could she be so blasé about screwing with my life? How could she accuse me of making the same mistake she had made over and over again? I pulled into Alice's front yard and jumped off my bike.

"Alice!" I called out as I banged on the door.

Just then, headlights filled the driveway as a car pulled in front of me. I squinted against the glare as Keith stepped out of his Lexus in all his button-down-shirt and relaxed-jeans glory. His sudden arrival caught me by surprise and was enough to make me momentarily forget all my problems with Barbie. (It was, quite frankly, enough to make me forget about everything.) "What are you doing here?" I asked.

"I just took Alice to Thelma's," he said. "She was worried that she had forgotten to lock the back door, so I told her I'd come back and check it."

"Alice called you and asked you to take her to Thelma's?" I said, surprised.

"I stopped by to ask her if she wanted me to trim her hedges this week, and she said she needed to go to Thelma's and she couldn't drive her car. Maybe there's something wrong with it." He shrugged and took a step closer. "Are you okay? You look upset."

"Yeah, I'm fine," I said, wiping my eyes.

He paused for a moment and then said, "Want to walk around back with me? I have to check that door."

I nodded and followed him around the side of the

house. The full moon reflected off the creek, cloaking everything in a soft, surreal glow.

"How was bingo?" he asked.

Bingo? It seemed like a million years ago. "Good," I said as he tugged on the door.

"Locked." He motioned toward the white patio chairs on the back porch. "Want to sit down for a minute?" he asked.

I shrugged and plopped down on the hard, cool plastic.

He took a seat beside me. "Are you sure you're okay?"

I sighed and said, "I just met my mother's boyfriend."

Keith winced. "Yikes. Not good, huh?"

I was so anxious I couldn't stop my teeth from chattering. "I just . . . I don't understand how my mother can do this. He has a wife."

"Maybe things with his wife aren't great."

I looked at him, surprised. Was he defending my mother's affair? "So what? It doesn't make it right. The woman is a professional home wrecker."

Keith sighed. "I don't know, Stef. I think it's more complicated than that. Maybe this guy hasn't been happy for a long time and when he met your mother, she made him realize just how unhappy he was."

"So why doesn't he divorce his wife?"

"Who knows? Perhaps he will."

I bowed my head in submission. "Great, then I'll have a cheater for a stepfather."

"That's pretty harsh. He could be a good guy. Maybe he didn't plan on any of this. Sometimes life just takes you by surprise, you know? You have everything all planned out, and then you meet someone and then crap happens."

The weird thing was that by the sound of Keith's voice, he didn't seem to be talking about my mother anymore. It felt as though he was talking about us.

"You don't understand," I said, looking up and returning his gaze. "She does this all the time. And she always gets hurt. I can't watch her do this to herself again."

He folded his hands behind his head. "Stef, from what little I know, your mom seems to take care of herself. Fresh starts aren't the worst thing in the world, right? She's just trying to find out what makes her happy."

"But she's not happy," I said. "It's like she has no impulse control or something. And you should see her when these affairs are over. She's a basket case. There have been times when I've been worried that she might actually hurt herself." I rubbed my eyes. I didn't want him to see me cry. "I can't stand by and watch her do this to herself again. I won't."

"So how do you plan on stopping her?"

"I don't know," I croaked.

"You can't save her, Stef," he said quietly.

"I have to at least try." I thought about my grandparents, and tears started cascading down my cheeks.

"Look, Stef, no matter what you do, it's just not going to make any difference in the long run. I know what I'm talking about. I tried to save my mother over and over again, and no matter what I did . . ." His voice faded. "You heard she died in a car accident, right?"

I nodded.

"Well, that's not the truth. My dad told people that for my sake, I guess. And for the insurance money too." He blinked a few times, as if he was trying to hold in all his emotions. "My mom killed herself."

I felt my breath catch in my throat. It was as if he had changed right in front of my eyes, morphing from a cliché hot lifeguard fantasy into a real person, a person who had been to hell and back and had lived to talk about it. And here he was, sharing it with me.

"It was . . . awful," he said after a long pause. He seemed to be remembering just how terrible it had been. It was obvious from the hoarse tone of his voice that this was difficult for him to talk about. "I knew she was depressed but I didn't think it was that bad. One morning I left for school, and that afternoon, instead of my mom picking me up, my dad was there. He told me she had driven down to the Potomac that morning and swallowed a bottle of sleeping pills. Her note said she wanted to die looking at the water. When she collapsed, the car shifted into neutral and slammed into a tree. So I guess he didn't tell a total lie. The actual cause of death was head injury."

I felt the urge to take him in my arms and hold him and tell him that everything would be all right. "That sucks," I said.

Pretty close.

"Yeah," he said, closing his eyes briefly as if trying to delete the memory. "It does." He glanced at me. "No one else knows that on the island. Besides Alice, of course. I don't think anyone can keep any secrets from her, do you?" He smiled.

Alice knew this? And she hadn't told me? That was so unlike her. These days she wasn't living up to her flawless status.

"So why did you tell me the truth?" I asked.

He smiled widely. "I had a feeling you would understand. Because your life hasn't been easy either."

In essence, Keith was saying that we were alike, but still, I felt as though he was much stronger than me. "I think losing someone you love is worse than anything I've had to endure. I mean, my dad died, but that happened before I was born."

"Any grandparents?" he asked.

I shook my head. "I have no idea who my dad's parents are, and my mom's died when she was in high school. They drowned in a freak catamaran accident. That's why I never learned how to swim. Barbie's been terrified of the water ever since."

"Yeah, well, losing one parent was enough to make

me a little crazy. Losing both at the same time has to be tough."

I thought about my mom and wondered how much of her love lunacy was due to waking up one morning and realizing that the two people she loved most in life were gone forever. "Barbie said that the one thing she learned when her parents died was that you have to live each day like it's your last," I said.

"So your mom has good advice sometimes," he said.

"I guess," I said with a shrug.

And then he reached out and took my hand in his. Keith had touched me many times before, but it had always been in the water, where he'd been acting more like an instructor. This felt completely different. I stared at his fingers, which were entwined with mine, and realized that this meant something big. And as terrified as I was of being eaten alive by love lunacy, I didn't want to let go.

So I didn't. Instead I squeezed his hand tightly and sat there with him, looking at the creek, imagining the grin that would have appeared on Alice's face if she had come home right then and seen us.

13

I woke up on Monday morning determined to cut Barbie some slack. All the sentimental dead mother stuff had made me realize how lucky I was to at least have a mother. And my love for Keith was proof that he was right, that sometimes "crap happens." So I was feeling extremely generous and forgiving, until I noticed that my whole *Funniest Animals* video collection had gone AWOL.

This was enough to make me forget about every nice thing that I had ever said or thought about my mother. I stormed out of my room, anxious for a confrontation. *How dare she?* She brought some strange guy home, paraded him in front of me, and then she actually had the gall to punish *me*? What had I done? (Besides the whole starting an argument and walking out on her thing.)

Unfortunately, Barbie wasn't there to scream at, so I

walk into her room, intent on revenge. I went through all her drawers, searching for something to hold hostage. I finally got a big plastic bag and threw all her lingerie into it. Then I stuffed the bag into my backpack and went to work.

When I got there, I had another surprise. Alice was cleaning the toilets in the ladies' locker room as if nothing weird had transpired the previous evening. She seemed perfectly fine too, not tired in the least.

"What happened to you last night?" I asked. "Why did you go Thelma's house?"

Alice continued to scrub the bowl with a long brush. "Thelma . . . wasn't feeling all that well. Must have been a bad wonton. Anyway, she asked me if I wouldn't mind coming over for a while."

"But why did you have Keith drive you?" This story sounded pretty suspicious.

"My car was acting up. How do you know I went to Thelma's?" She sounded as irritated as Barbie did when I gave her the third degree.

"Because I went over to your house last night and I ran into Keith when he came to check on the door."

Alice stopped scrubbing and gave me her full attention. "You came over last night?"

I nodded. "Barbie's boyfriend was at the apartment when I got home."

"Oh, Stef," Alice said sympathetically. And I could tell from the look in her eyes that she knew without my saying anything else just how terrible it had been. "I'm sorry I wasn't there for you."

"That's all right," I said. A smirk crept across my face. "Keith was there." And then while Alice took a seat on a sparkling clean toilet, I told her everything.

When I was finished, Alice was grinning. "He's really special, Steffie."

"I know," I replied. And then I told her what I was pretty sure she already knew. "I think I love him."

Of course, this was all before I saw Keith making out with Mora.

Until 5:30 p.m. things had really been looking up. I had a backpack full of my mother's lingerie, I'd had a nice heart-to-heart with Alice, and I had gone palm to palm with the greatest guy in all of Maryland.

I had left work feeling like I was on top of the world, humming at the top of my lungs. I couldn't help noticing that the world actually seemed brighter, as if it had gotten happier right along with me. The grass was greener, the birds more colorful. Even the stone Adonis in the fountain looked fulfilled. It was as if the entire world was rejoicing at my and Keith's progress.

I walked to my bike and paused. That was my big mistake. Instead of just moving the kickstand and riding away, I glanced toward the pool to see if I could spot Keith. And I saw him all right, except not at the pool. He was with Mora, off to the side of the pool in a secluded area so thick with shrubbery that the golfers referred to it as the woods. They were smashed against each other, chest to chest and cheek to cheek. Keith was running his fingers through her hair and appeared to be whispering into her ear.

It was enough to send me spiraling back to this dismal place people referred to as Earth. I felt as if I might actually lose the baloney sandwich Alice had made me for lunch. The ride home was a blur of self-recrimination. After all, I had been through this a million times with Barbie. I should've known better than to pin my hopes on a guy who belonged to someone else.

When I stormed into the apartment, I prayed that my mom would be off with Ludwig somewhere so I could go to my room and sob in peace. But there she was, sprawled out on the couch in her bathrobe and blowing her nose as if she had the flu or something. Her eyes were red and puffy, and her mascara was smeared and running down her face.

Oh no.

"Tom is such a jackass!" she exclaimed, waving a tissue around in the air.

Apparently, this was replacing "hello" in the Rogers household.

Barbie choked up some phlegm. "He said he needed time to think. Can you believe it? He said seeing you last night made him realize that there were other people's lives at stake here, not just him and me."

"Are you pinning this on me?" I began to bawl. My

overwhelming dismay was enough to make Barbie stop crying. Not that I was dense enough to expect my mom to be there for me in my time of need, but I really couldn't handle being blamed for the end of her relationship when in reality I had just been in the wrong place at the wrong time.

"Of course not," she said. "He's just a jackass." She got up and kissed my forehead. "I'm sorry, Steffie. I'm so sorry for everything. You were right. He was a jerk and I had no right to bring him into our home."

"That's not why I'm so upset!" I was panting more heavily than a greyhound on a racetrack. "I just saw Keith and Mora making out."

"Oh no!" my mom shrieked. After all, if anyone could understand how terrible it was to see the man I was planning on making my soul mate in the arms of his betrothed, it was my mother. "What happened?" She handed me her box of tissues.

"They were kissing in the woods by Tippecanoe." I grabbed a tissue and blew my nose. "It wouldn't have been so bad if I hadn't just been with him last night."

Barbie looked confused. "Last night? I thought you were at bingo."

"After I saw you with, well, the jackass, I went over to Alice's house, but she wasn't home. Keith showed up and we started talking, and, well, one thing led to another and . . ." I hesitated.

My mother's eyes grew as big as saucers and she

dropped her tissue. "You did it?" she whispered. And then she screeched: "Please tell me you had enough common sense to use protection!"

"*No!*" I shouted, horrified that Barbie was even thinking what she was thinking.

My mother held a hand to her chest and fell backward on the couch. "I'm so not ready to be a grandmother," she said.

"For God's sake, Barbie. I haven't even kissed him. We held hands."

"Held hands?" she asked. "That's all you did?" Was it my imagination, or did she sound disappointed?

"Yeah," I said. "I mean, he told me stuff that no one else knows. I thought it meant something. Something big."

"Jackass!" my mom exclaimed.

"But he's not." I flopped down next to her. "At least, I didn't think so. He seemed so sweet, you know? So sincere."

Barbie sighed and shook her head. "They're all the same."

But were they? Or was it just my mother and I who were the same?

"How could I have been so stupid?" I asked out loud.

"Honey," my mom said, "I've been asking myself that very question all day."

"But it really seemed like he cared about me."

"Tell me about it."

"I never want to talk to him again," I announced.

"I feel the same way," Barbie said.

All of a sudden, the phone rang and we both jumped. *Jumped*. She scrambled for her cell, me for the landline. Mother-and-daughter hot-potato phone.

Although it was for me (obvious, since we were not being serenaded by Beethoven), I didn't pick up. Instead, I hovered over the answering machine, listening as Keith said something had "come up" and he couldn't make our lesson that night.

Afterward, Barbie said, "You would've gone to him if he'd asked you, wouldn't you? Even after seeing him with his girlfriend."

I wasn't sure. I knew one thing for certain, though: I would've traded anything to go back in time and relive the previous night.

Barbie shook her head. "See, Stef? It's not always easy to walk away."

That was when it occurred to me: once upon a time, my mom was just like me. She probably fell for a guy with a girlfriend, and before she knew it, it was neither the guy nor the girlfriend who was consuming her, but the disease of love lunacy. And if I wasn't careful, I would end up like her, sitting on an old couch in a crappy apartment, next to my fatherless daughter, who was showing signs of inheriting the family illness.

But I was not my mother. And I wanted to prove it to myself somehow.

First I went into her room and dumped all her lingerie back in her drawer. Next I went back into my room and put my swimsuit on under my clothes. And then I told my mom I needed to get some fresh air.

I rode my bike to Crab Beach, took off my clothes, and waded in until the warm water was up to my waist.

I wished that at that moment I had plunged in and glided gracefully out to sea, but the truth of the matter was, I was too scared to try to swim by myself. So I backed up and sat down, the water rising to my shoulders. I stayed there until the sun set and I thought I felt something slimy touch my arm. And then I jumped up, put my clothes back on, and rode home, thinking, *I'm not my mother*.

At least not yet.

14

Ways to handle a cheating man:

1) Toss a drink in his face and walk away. (From the way Barbie described it, the merlot debacle was the harshest thing anyone had ever done to her, which is why I thought it was cool.)
2) Make a big public scene in which you accuse him of infidelity at the top of your lungs. (Which will pretty much assure that you'll never see him again.)
3) Cheat on him. (What's good for the goose is good for the gander, whatever that means.)
4) Drop him.

If someone had forced me to choose, I would have preferred number one followed by number two. But unfortunately, none of these options really fitted my predicament. Because technically, Keith wasn't cheating on me. He was cheating on Mora. And even that was a huge leap in logic because we hadn't done anything but swim (sort of) and hold hands.

So I really didn't know what I was going to do when, the very next morning, he walked right up to me (when I was polishing the brass railing in the main lobby) with a big smile on his face as if everything was totally cool and nothing weird had happened whatsoever.

"Hey," he said cheerfully.

Even though he was looking amazing as per usual (red swim trunks + white T-shirt + flip-flops + shiny whistle dangling around the neck = very, *very* sexy), his entire demeanor unnerved me. Wasn't he supposed to feel the slightest bit guilty for leading me on?

"Sorry I had to cancel yesterday. Do you want to get together tonight?" he asked.

I could feel my willpower fading, but I shook my head and continued polishing. "I can't."

"Oh." He scratched his head. "All right. How about tomorrow?"

Suddenly, a little voice in my head started talking and it was saying things like: *Maybe he wasn't really making out with Mora. Maybe you didn't see what you thought you saw. Maybe he was giving her CPR or something.*

"Sorry, Keith, I'm busy," I forced myself to say. No

way. I was not going to believe any of the ridiculous excuses I was so willing to provide. Why would Mora need CPR in the woods?

"What do you mean 'busy'?" He sounded annoyed.

"I mean I can't, so just . . . leave me alone," I said quickly, before turning away and sprinting into the girls' locker room, where Alice was more than ready to give me a big bear hug.

"Well, I did it," I whispered. "I dropped him." And then I burst into tears, because getting over love lunacy hurts really, really bad.

I managed to avoid Keith for the rest of the day, which drained me of every single bit of energy and resolve. I wasn't sure if I had the strength to stay away from him. I hated to admit it, but I was starting to understand why my mother wanted to move every time a relationship ended. I didn't think I could handle seeing Keith with Mora again. If it hadn't been for Alice and the fact that Keith was leaving to go back to college soon, I would've yanked out the map of Maryland and done the finger drop myself.

After work, I rode home. As I pedaled into our apartment parking lot, I caught sight of Keith's black Lexus. There he was, waiting for me on the steps, appearing very out of sorts. I tried to walk right by him, but he grabbed me by the wrist and I stopped in my tracks.

"Can I talk to you?" he asked.

I swallowed hard and kept quiet.

Keith sighed in frustration. "Stef, what's going on?"

"What do you mean?" I wasn't trying to be coy, really. But I was stuck in panic mode and I couldn't think of anything else to say.

He glanced away. "You didn't strike me as the type to play games."

Excuuuuse me? Wasn't that the pot calling the kettle black? "Look," I said. "I just can't do this."

Keith's eyes fixed on mine. "Do what?"

"This," I said with a shrug. "Talking to you and, well, being with you."

He crossed his arms in front of his chest, as if he was protecting himself or something. "Why?"

"Because I don't want to be the other woman. It's not fair to me."

"I don't want you to be the other woman either."

"Oh," I mumbled. I could feel my heart twisting into a fisherman's knot. Here I was, spending all this time thinking Keith was into me, when in actuality, he obviously thought of me as his first cousin. "I thought that when you held my hand last night, that meant you were, well, interested."

Keith's lips turned up into a smile. "But I am interested."

Whoa. This was *huge.* He'd just admitted to liking me-liking me. But wait, didn't he remember that other-woman thing?

"Keith, I'm interested too, but I can't have all these heart-to-heart talks and stuff and then watch you make out with your girlfriend," I said firmly. "It's just . . . weird."

His face became all pinched. "What are you talking about?"

I rolled my eyes. "I saw you guys in the woods."

He squinted as if he was in deep thought. Apparently, there were so many times to choose from, he couldn't figure out when I had caught him.

And then I could almost see the lightbulb turn on over his head. "So that's what this is all about," he said, chuckling.

I felt the need to be sarcastic. Like, *Oh yeah—can you imagine? I had a problem with that!*

He put his hands on my shoulders. "Can I come in and explain?"

I was tempted to leave everything as it was. How many excuses could a guy have? However, for the sake of curiosity, I invited him inside.

When we sat down on the ghetto couch together, he said, "It wasn't what you think. Mora and I broke up."

The knot in my heart tightened, and for a split second I was pretty sure I was going to need some of that CPR Keith was so good at.

Keith went on. "She's not handling this all that well. What you saw in the woods was nothing more than me comforting her."

I replayed the scene of him and Mora in the woods in my mind again. Huh. The truth was, I had not seen any real lip-to-lip contact. Actually, I had not even seen Mora's face. What I had seen was Mora nestling her head against his shoulder while he held her tight. Wow, he was telling the truth.

"Is that why you couldn't get together last night?" I asked. "Were you with Mora?"

He sighed. "Like I said, this whole thing has hit her pretty hard. She knew I wasn't happy, but I guess she thought we'd work it out somehow. Her parents weren't around last night, and I felt funny about leaving her alone while she was so upset."

And then he took my hand again. This time his palm was kind of sweaty. He must have been nervous. I couldn't get over it. Keith was nervous around *me*? I was expecting the whole universe to cave in.

"Look, Stef, I like you. I want to get to know you." He paused, as if he was trying to reorganize his thoughts. "I'll be going back to school soon, but I'd like to spend as much time as possible with you before then." He squeezed my hand gently as my whole body went almost limp. "How does that sound?"

I couldn't speak. There were no words for how I was feeling just then.

Keith took his other hand and brushed it down the side of my face, his fingers tracing the outline of my chin. He leaned forward and I inhaled as if I was about to snorkel or something. And then we were kissing. It was slow and soft, like we wanted to savor every second that it lasted. I wrapped my arms around his neck and pulled him closer. He smelled like Irish Spring and tasted like peppermint patties, and he felt tender and strong at the same time.

Finally, we both broke for air and we sat there together, breathing raggedly with our heads touching and our arms around each other. Keith's smile was enormous. And mine was so big my cheeks were hurting.

"You and I should go out tonight," he said.

"An official date?"

"Official," he said.

"Knock, knock." My mother appeared in the doorway. "I hope I'm not interrupting anything." She raised an eyebrow in my direction and winked, making it clear that she understood exactly what she had interrupted.

"Actually, I was just leaving," Keith said. He picked himself up off the couch, turned back toward me, and grinned. "I'll pick you up at eight-thirty."

I could only manage a nod.

After he left, Barbie perched herself on the arm of the sofa and said smugly, "Well, well, well."

I grabbed a pillow and put it behind my neck. "It's not what you think."

"Really? Because I think you just accepted a date

with the same boy who was lip-locked with Mora twenty-four hours ago."

"He broke up with her."

"Congratulations!" she said proudly. "And I have some wonderful news, too. Tom asked his wife for a divorce!" She held out her arms for a hug.

"What?" I said as my mother smashed me up against her hard boobs.

"He said our little tiff made him realize how much he truly loved me. He said he wants to spend as much time as possible just getting to know me."

"He said that?" The feeling of elation in my chest tightened into a feeling of pure anxiety. It was a coincidence, I reassured myself. Just because Keith had said practically the same thing to me didn't mean my relationship with him was anything like my mother's relationship with . . . the jackass.

"Look at us," my mother said, oblivious to my distress. "Last night we were both in a funk, thinking we had lost the guys we loved, and now tonight, here we are." She grinned as she released me. "And I've got even better news for you. Tom is taking me away this weekend to celebrate. So you'll have the apartment to yourself. You know what that means?"

I gave her a confused look. "I get to watch whatever I want on TV?"

My mother laughed. I wasn't really joking, however.

"Come with me." She motioned toward the bathroom, and I followed her. She opened up the closet and reached into a cosmetics bag. "Here's where I keep the condoms."

Maybe there were some girls out there who would have appreciated knowing where their mothers kept their birth control, but I was not one of them.

"If you want," Barbie continued, "next week we can take you and get you fitted for a diaphragm or get you a prescription for the pill, whichever you prefer. The diaphragm can be a hassle because you have to insert it right before, and sometimes it's hard to stop after you've gotten started, but, well, if you don't, you get a Steffie or something that requires antibiotics."

Oh, ew.

I pushed away the cosmetics bag in disgust. "I'm not going to need those, Barbie."

"This Keith of yours isn't as innocent as you'd like to think, Stef. He's been around and around and back again." This sounded more like a warning and less like motherly advice, but I was going to stand my ground. Keith and I had a lot of bases to cover before we could even consider, as Alice would have put it, parking the pastrami.

"I'm not having sex this weekend," I said.

She rolled her eyes. "Well, *if* you do," she said, as if certain I would, "you know where the protection is."

"Great," I said through a heavy sigh. "I'm going to Alice's."

Barbie blew me an air kiss as I galloped to the front door. "Call me on my cell if you need anything!"

I didn't want to hurt her feelings, but really, if I'd needed something, she would have been the last person I would have called.

I hadn't made any plans to see Alice, but I was dying to tell her about the latest Keith developments, and I really couldn't stand to be in my mother's "I heart Planned Parenthood" company for another second. So I pedaled to her house as fast as I could. It was officially the second week in August. The heat was easing up once night fell, and the light breeze felt good on my skin. It felt even better knowing that because Keith and Mora weren't together anymore, I no longer needed to be concerned about love lunacy. He was free to be loved by anyone now, and that anyone was definitely me.

But my Keith McKnight high disappeared when I pulled into Alice's driveway. Usually when she was home, she'd leave her door wide open. Now, even though her car was in the driveway, her door was shut.

"Alice!" I called out. I knocked on the door a few times and when she didn't respond, I walked around back to see if she was in her yard. I was just about to leave when I glanced inside. Alice was lying on the living room couch. I knocked on the window.

"Steffie," she said, waving me inside. "What a nice surprise."

"Are you all right?" I asked as I sat down next to her. After all, not only was the house dark and about a million degrees, but also, Alice was covered in a blanket.

"Fine." She pushed herself up to make more room for me. "I'm just tired, that's all."

She looked at me and tilted her head. "What's going on?" she asked. "Why do you look so flushed?"

And then I did the most ridiculous teenybopper thing in the entire world. I started bouncing up and down on Alice's couch like I was professing my love on *Oprah*.

Alice didn't look very amused, though. "Quit it, Stef. One more bounce and this thing is going to crumble like a cookie."

Then I began giggling like a maniac. "Keith broke up with Mora!" I shouted.

Alice grinned widely. "Well, it's about time."

"Keith kissed me!" I screamed.

She plugged her ears. "Are you going to yell again?"

I smiled and sat down next to her. "No, I'm done."

"Good," Alice replied. And then she threw her blanket up into the air, dragged herself off the couch, and did a little dance on her sunflower rug. "This is the Steffie-finally-got-some jig!" she exclaimed.

"Can I join you?" I asked, reaching for the remote to her stereo.

"You better," she said, chuckling. "Before I dislocate my hip."

I blasted a cheesy Gwen Stefani song, and Alice and I got our boogie on like we were in the finals on *Dancing with the Stars*. After a few minutes of doing some oldies moves—including the swim—we collapsed on the floor, laughing like there was no tomorrow.

"I don't see how it could get any better," Alice said simply as the music died down.

And she was right. But it was about to get worse.

15

I have always loved a happy ending. And what could be better than the geeky girl hooking up with the most popular stud in town? Unfortunately for me, however, I was not living in a Disney movie. So instead of dressing in a ballroom gown and celebrating the grand finale by having dinner on some rooftop balcony overlooking the sparkling city lights, I wore one of my mother's Forever 21 sundresses and dined in a dingy-looking Ethiopian restaurant in a Stevensville strip mall. And instead of sipping bubbly while my prince fed me tiny bites of filet mignon, I gulped down my water as I tried my best to eat what appeared to be a platter of ground-up regurgitated baby food.

But regardless of the odd scenery or the bizarre meal I was eating, I was still with Keith, the fabulous fantasy guy I had fallen for fifty-six days before. Only now, what we had was becoming so real, it was actually kind of freaking me out.

"What do you think?" Keith asked after I had forced myself to taste all the dollops.

What I thought was that this was not exactly the kind of wholesome all-American food one would get at the China Buffet. However, I gazed into his shining eyes and reminded myself how great it was that he wore a sport jacket and tie, so I peeled off a big piece of wet bread and went for another dunk. "I think it's great," I said.

He smiled and took a short sip of his water. "I knew you'd like it."

Obviously, I was not presenting my true self, but I didn't care. I could tell from the grin on his face that he seemed to like this Ethiopian-food-lover me. And as Alice would have said, "If it ain't broke, don't fix it."

Keith took a hunk of bread and swiped it across the plate. We were nearing the conclusion of the meal, and all the portions were beginning to run into each other, achieving the impossible: it looked even worse than it had when it arrived at the table. But besides the food, things had been going great. We had shared a couple of quick but supersweet pecks on the way over to dinner. He had bought me some really pretty daffodils and opened the car door for me. I was all about this Boy Scout vibe of Keith's. I felt so taken care of, like I was the priority. The one person in my life who was supposed to be doing that was too busy with love lunacy to oblige.

"I come here a lot with my dad and stepmother," he said with his mouth full.

Even his bad table manners were hot.

I gulped some Diet Dr Pepper to chase down the taste of *iab* (I didn't find out until later that it was cottage cheese blended with yogurt.) "Do you get along with your stepmother?"

"Sort of. She's only fifteen years older than me, so it's not as though she and I have a mother-son relationship or anything like that. She pretty much leaves me alone."

Usher's "Yeah!" rang out from Keith's cell phone. "It's my dad," he said to me, snapping his phone open. "Uh-huh, right. Okay. Well, I'm sorry about that. Look, I . . ." His voice faded as he looked at me. "I can't talk about this right now. If she calls back, tell her I'll speak to her later. I've got to go," he said. "That's my other line." He clicked over. "Hello?"

The expression on his face changed, and I knew without a doubt that the caller on the other line was none other than Mora. I finished the rest of my Dr Pepper with one mighty swig and let out a tiny burp that thankfully he didn't hear.

"Hey," he said softly.

My lower extremities immediately went numb. I

knew that up until, well, yesterday, she had been a big part of his life, but I really resented the intrusion. I wished I could've closed my eyes and gone back in time. I wished that we had moved to Jones Island years ago and that I had got to him first. I wished that I could tear that phone away from his ear and throw it in the restaurant's saltwater aquarium.

"Yeah, well, okay, calm down," I heard him say.

I wondered how many of these one-sided conversations my mom had endured. I wondered how many times she had been filled with the weird jealous feeling that came with realizing that the man you loved still belonged to someone else. Fourteen at least, I supposed. I couldn't imagine feeling this insecure and uncomfortable over and over and over again. Once was enough.

"I have to go." His eyes shifted to me. "I'll talk to you later." He flashed me a kind of sad-looking smile as he turned off his phone. "Sorry about that."

"That's okay," I said, even though it wasn't.

"No, it's not," he said. "I wouldn't have picked up if I'd known it was her. I'm sorry to put you in that position."

"I already knew that breakups were messy," I said, reaching across the table and taking his hand.

He stroked the inside of my wrist with his thumb. "It's just made worse by the fact that Mora's parents and my parents are friends. Everyone feels the need to add their two cents."

"That's got to be hard," I said stiffly. Truth of the matter was, I didn't want to talk about Mora anymore. Nor did I want to talk about how upset Keith's parents were that he'd broken up with her. I just wanted him and me to have a fresh start, where there was no baggage or past lives and there would only be us.

"Yeah, well, thanks for being so understanding." He brought my hand up to his mouth and kissed it softly. (Wow!) "Are you ready to get out of here, cutie?"

Cutie was born ready.

Keith paid the bill with his very own ultraplatinum credit card (even though I offered to split it—he was such a gentleman) and we climbed back into his Lexus.

"Where to?" He put his right hand on my knee and then brought it slowly up my thigh.

"We could go back to my apartment," I said abruptly. "Barbie's out of town for the weekend." This wasn't the most subtle of suggestions. But all I knew was that I wanted to do whatever it took to make him forget all about his ex-girlfriend. I wanted to prove to him that Mora was not the girl for him. I was.

"Okay," he said, and then he leaned in and kissed me tenderly.

As we drove, I put my head back and closed my eyes. I attempted to calm the jackhammering in my stomach by taking deep breaths of the musky leather-scented car air. I wasn't sure what was about to happen, but whatever it was, I was ready. I loved Keith, he liked (potentially loved) me. It was all coming together.

Keith stopped the car. When I opened my eyes, I saw that we weren't at my apartment. We were at the entrance to Crab Beach.

"What are we doing?" I asked. "I thought we were going back to my place."

A mischievous look appeared on Keith's face. "We are. But first, we're going swimming."

Swimming? "I don't have my suit," I said.

"I know," he said with a wink.

My heart slammed against my chest like a crash-test dummy against a brick wall. He wanted to go *skinny-dipping?* Even though just minutes earlier I had been considering going all the way with him, I was possessed with a panic so intense, it was amazing I was still conscious.

I made a quick mental list of all thoughts spinning through my mind:

1) *Holy crap.*
2) *Barbie was right. He's not innocent at all.*
3) *Am I wearing my spanky pants or my good bikinis?*

My panic must have been obvious, because Keith grinned and said, "We can wear underwear if you want, Stef. No pressure."

"I think it would be better," I said. "After all, I don't want any fish . . ." My voice drifted off. Fish to do what? What exactly was I worried that the "fish" might do? "You know," I added, as if that summed it up.

Keith popped open the trunk and pulled out two thick white towels emblazoned with the Tippecanoe Country Club insignia. He took my hand and led me down to the beach. He dropped the towels and wasted no time in yanking off his jacket, shirt, and tie.

Okay, so we were just going to strip right there. I could handle it. After all, even though I was wearing my matching bikini set (I had peeked, just to make sure), it still covered just as much as a bikini. Right?

I pulled off my crocheted cardigan as Keith kicked off his khakis. I was happy to see he was a boxer, not a brief guy. I hated watching those reality shows where they had a really cute guy and suddenly they'd show him getting ready for bed and he'd be wearing, like, skanky black bikinis or tightie whities or something. I was supersmitten with Keith, but I would've had a hard time getting over little black bikinis. In any case, I didn't have to worry. Keith wore those white boxer-briefs that were kind of thick and snug, so in reality (I reassured myself), they covered just as much as his suit did.

I unwrapped the tie on my dress and slipped it off. There I was, standing in front of Keith McKnight in my matching light blue underwear that my mom had tucked into my stocking at Christmas.

He took my hand and nodded toward the water. "Come on."

We walked in together, and when the water was up to our waists, Keith let go of my hand and dove in.

He popped up a few feet away and held out his hand to me. "Don't be frightened, Stef."

The words alone were enough to make me melt. Not to mention the way he was staring at me.

"Let's see what you remember," he added, giving me a nod of encouragement.

And that's where the movie moment ended. Because even though I plunged right in, it was not a graceful move. My swimming was all discombobulated, kind of like the doggy-paddle desperate-to-stay-above-the-water stroke. Not pretty in the least. In fact, highly embarrassing would have been the best way to describe it.

He caught me under my arms and lifted me out of the water. Holding me tightly against him, he said, "Look up."

It was a full moon and the sky was littered with stars. There weren't any clouds either, just a streak of constellations showering us with light. "I used to come here at night as a kid. I would strip down and just float on my back for hours, staring up at the stars."

"It sounds . . . incredible," I said breathlessly.

"Just focus on the stars," he whispered into my ear. "The water will hold you."

I stepped away from him. I looked up. I leaned back,

resting my head on the top of the water as if it was a pillow. I felt my feet slowly rise toward the surface. But I didn't think about my feet, I didn't think about anything but the stars. And I floated. All by myself. I was vaguely aware of Keith drifting beside me, and every now and then our hands would brush up against each other. But neither of us said a word.

Suddenly, I realized that Keith was no longer floating. He was standing beside me, looking down at me with this hint of wonder in his eye that made me feel like I was special.

"Time to go," he said, and helped me to my feet. He led me back to shore and we wrapped the towels around ourselves and gathered up our clothes. We drove back to my apartment in silence, as if we were both anticipating the possibilities.

He parked the car and followed me into my apartment. Considering that both of us were in our underwear with nothing but towels wrapped around us, I was more than grateful we had not run into our neighbor Herbert Lewis. That would have been a big buzz kill.

When we got inside, I turned on the light next to the couch. What was I supposed to do now? I thought back to that lawn mowing day at Alice's. "Do you, um . . . want something to drink?"

Keith fidgeted with his towel. "Sure. What have you got?"

I went into the kitchen and opened the refrigerator.

The only thing to drink was my mother's grody melon coolers (they tasted remarkably similar to the cough syrup in our medicine cabinet) and three cans of diet Pepsi.

"I'll just have water," he said.

I poured him a glass and handed it to him.

"Are you all right?" he asked, motioning toward my shaking hand.

"Sure," I said with half a laugh. But there was nothing funny about this situation. Nothing at all.

He ran his finger down the side of my face and neck. "Don't be nervous," he said. And then he gave me a soft, slow, passionate kiss. He stopped and smiled. "Come on." He took my hand and pulled me onto the couch. Then he put his arm around me and leaned over me, kissing me again and again.

He started getting more intense and nuzzling my neck. My thoughts were spiraling out of control. *This is it. Any minute he's going to be reaching under my towel. And after that, there isn't that much to take off to be completely naked. So when should I break for the condoms? Will he be offended if I ask him to wear one? What if he refuses? Because there is no way I am doing it without one. Not that I am so worried about diseases because, even though maybe I should be, I am more worried about getting pregnant. Because my mom has jinxed me. And I am not about to risk getting pregnant at only seventeen. . . .*

"Stef," he murmured. "Is there something wrong?"

I opened my eyes. He was no longer kissing me but

looking at me with concern. This would've been a good time to tell him I was afraid. But afraid of what? Love lunacy? He'd never comprehend what any of it meant, and now that Mora wasn't involved with him anymore, love lunacy seemed to be a nonissue. Actually, it became all too evident that what I really was terrified of was, quite simply, love. The idea of making some of it with Keith when Barbie and I were on the brink of a finger move and he was about to go back to college was truly sending me headfirst into a nervous breakdown. I had to put a stop to this, and quick.

"We're going too fast!" I announced loudly.

"That's okay." He wrapped his arms around me and kissed me on my forehead. "I don't want to do anything you don't feel ready for."

Instead of easing my troubled mind, this comment touched an exposed nerve. I was so mad at myself for this. I was the one who'd asked Keith back to my apartment, which was pretty much sign language for "Sleep with me, you big hunk of man!" And I'd done that for one reason—to seduce him and make him forget about Mora. But now Keith's ex-girlfriend was in every thought of mine, and in every thought she was in bed with Keith. I was so jealous I could barely see straight.

"Did you have sex with Mora?" I asked bluntly.

The words hung in the air, catching us both by surprise.

He glanced away and stood up. "Why don't you get

dressed," he said. But it wasn't really a question. It was more like a command.

I walked into the bedroom, feeling devastated. Why had I ruined a perfectly wonderful moment with my big fat mouth?

When I came out (wearing my SAVE THE BAY T-shirt and running shorts), he was sitting on the couch reading Barbie's *In Touch* magazine. He looked really puzzled, but I doubted it had anything to do with Brangelina's love child.

"Regarding Mora," he said softly. "Do you really want to know?"

The truth was I didn't really want to know. What I wanted to hear was that they hadn't been together and he hadn't seen her naked and he hadn't experienced any earth-shattering sex with her. But I had a feeling that they had.

Keith took my silence as an affirmation. "Look, Mora and I were friends for a long time. Neither one of us was seeing anyone last summer and, well, things just happened."

And just like that, I became enraged. Not upset or sad, but enraged. It was completely irrational and I knew I was wrong to feel that way, but I couldn't help it. Which is why I took my anger out on him.

"So what you're telling me is just because you were bored and needed a partner for Parcheesi, you decided to go over and de-virginize Mora?"

His cheek muscles tightened. I had definitely crossed a line with him. "De-virginize?"

"That's what Doris said," I added with a shrug. I figured if I was going down, I might as well drag one of my friends with me.

"This isn't about Mora, is it?"

"What else would this be about?" My voice was filled with contempt, and I could tell by Keith's stiff posture that he wasn't pleased with me at all.

"I have no idea, Stef. You're not really being forthcoming right now," he replied tersely.

"Well, how's this for forthcoming? I don't like being poor."

This was turning into a nightmare. I wanted to press Stop and Rewind, but the remote for my brain was obviously on the fritz.

"What are you talking about?" He was looking at me like I had suddenly started speaking Swahili.

"You said that I was like Alice. That I didn't care about money. Well, that's not true. Money makes the world go round, Keith. You should know. You've got so much of it, you can do whatever you want."

Keith stared at me. "Okay."

Okay? That was it? If this was Barbie, I totally would have baited her into a fight by now. But Keith wasn't going to sink to my extremely pathetic level. That didn't stop me from carrying on, though.

"And I don't like bugs either!" There. Take that.

"What are you doing, Stef?" He looked so sad, like I had hurt his feelings *and* attacked his dog with a weed whacker.

"I just . . . ," I began. Then I sighed. "I don't know."

Keith stood up. "I don't know either. But whatever it is, I don't like it."

I couldn't have agreed with him more.

He made his way toward the door. "I thought that once I cleared up this whole Mora thing we'd be fine."

I couldn't speak. I was still in shock from the fact that we had gone from getting together to breaking up in one day. And it was all my fault.

"Looks like I was wrong," he said sternly. Then he left without saying goodbye.

16

Steffie Rogers's advice on how not to get over the loss of a love:

1) Immediately after breaking up, go out for some "fresh air" and end up at the convenience store, where you purchase a six-pack of Jolt cola, a Snickers bar, and a quart of strawberry ice cream.

2) Go home and eat the ice cream right out of the container and then realize too late that you've just consumed the entire quart by yourself.

3) Wash the ice cream down with that six-pack of Jolt cola.

4) Pound your pillow.

5) Watch a gross TV show about plastic surgery that is sure to give you nightmares (if only you could sleep), and then eat the Snickers bar.

6) Repeatedly check your machine for messages

even though you've been sitting beside it the whole time (except for the ten minutes it took you to go to the convenience store).

7) Pick up the phone to call your ex. Dial his/her number. Hang up before anybody answers. Repeat.

8) Go to bed, where you toss and turn and wonder if anyone has ever died from consuming too much caffeine and sugar.

9) Go over every single line of dialogue you and your never-had-a-chance-to-be-boyfriend/girlfriend had, just so you can remember exactly how dumb you sounded.

10) Remember all the fun times you and he/she had (as well as the fun times you might have had, if you had only possessed enough common sense to keep your mouth shut).

The next morning I showed up at Tippecanoe not only miserable but also tired, bloated, and a little bit shaky. But I didn't care. I was anxious to be with Alice. I knew I'd feel better as soon as I told her what had happened.

I had just punched in my time card when the staff room door flew open. My heart lifted a little when I thought it might be Alice, but it sank once I realized it was Doris. And the second I looked at her puffy tear-stained face, I knew she was about to tell me the worst news I'd ever heard in my life.

"Steffie!" Doris cried. "Alice is in the hospital."

I had just read in the morning edition of the Jones Island paper about how when tragedy struck, people always said, "The day began like any other day . . ." But today hadn't begun just like any other day—at least, not for me. Therefore, according to the laws of the universe, nothing really horrible should have happened to me.

But it had. I dashed to Warthog's office and told him the news, and surprisingly the jerk let me take a personal day. Doris and I hopped into her car and she began updating me on the situation. I was so upset that I heard only every other sentence. Thelma had taken Alice to the hospital when she complained of being short of breath. . . . Alice was scheduled for heart surgery tomorrow. . . . She hadn't been feeling well for a long time.

Doris veered her car from one side of the road to the other. (Like Alice, Doris was a notoriously bad driver.) "I told her she needed to go to a doctor, but dammit, she was too stubborn. Even after the other night when we were all out to dinner and she got so sick, she refused to go. What did she do instead? She went to Thelma's house! What did she think Thelma would do if her heart stopped beating?"

Everything seemed so surreal, like I was having a really bad dream. Like I would wake up and find that I was sitting in Alice's backyard, with my feet in the baby pool. Alice and I would laugh, and she would pick up her notebook and we would entertain ourselves by making a list about what our wills would look like if we were worth millions of dollars.

"Why didn't she tell me?" I asked, trying to hold back my tears.

Doris sighed. "She didn't want to worry you, honey. She thought you had enough on your plate."

And suddenly I felt guilty. Maybe if I hadn't been so caught up in my own ridiculous life I would've noticed that Alice was really sick. Maybe I would've had enough sense to cancel my date with Keith and stay with Alice. Maybe I could've prevented this whole thing.

Doris and I parked the car in the St. Agnes Hospital parking lot and bolted inside. We received our visitor passes, got into the elevator, and went up to the fifth floor. When the doors opened, I took a few steps forward and stopped dead in my tracks. Keith was standing in front of me. I was too out of sorts to really freak out about running into him after our Chernobyl of a date. There were much more important things to be worried about. Still, my fingers went numb at the sight of him and the memory of how amazing his lips had felt against mine.

"Hey," I mumbled.

"Hi," he replied.

I noticed his eyes were bloodshot, like he had been crying.

"What are you doing here?" I asked.

"Visiting Alice," he said as he slipped his sunglasses on.

"Is she okay?"

Keith gulped a few times, as if he was trying to restrain himself from breaking down. The only thing he did was shrug, and then he stepped inside the elevator, waving meekly as the doors slid shut.

I was on my way to becoming a basket case.

But before I could completely lose it, Doris grabbed my arm and I followed her down the hall, trying really hard to ignore the nauseating frog-in-formaldehyde stench that seemed to permeate all hospitals. I walked into Alice's room and stopped in my tracks. This was not the cheerful, light-filled space depicted on *General Hospital*. Medical equipment was everywhere, and the room, with its gray tiled floor and dingy white walls, looked as dismal as a scene from one of Alice's old black-and-white movies.

"Steffie," Alice said with a smile, pushing herself up in bed. Thelma, who was sitting in a chair beside Alice's bed, reading an old edition of *Glamour*, gave me a little wave before focusing back on her magazine.

Until then I had done a good job of holding it together. There had been no crying jags or dramatic proclamations like "What if she doesn't make it?" or "I'll never have a better friend!" But when I saw tough little Alice wearing that hideous blue hospital gown, and lying in that bed with an IV running into her arm, and hooked up to a bleeping heart monitor, I could feel myself start to break down at the thought of losing her forever or even for just a day.

"Don't cry, honey." Alice was the picture of calm. She held out her hand. "I'm going to be okay, really."

I took her hand in mine. "So, what happened? Did you have a heart attack?"

"No, no," Alice said dismissively. "Nothing like that. It's just that my heart valve isn't working properly. . . ."

"Mitral valve prolapse," Doris said authoritatively.

Alice rolled her eyes and smiled at me. "They're going to fix my mitral valve."

"How do they do that?" I asked.

"Well, they stop your heart, take it right out of you, and fix it," said Doris, making an X over her heart.

The image of an Inca warrior holding a still-beating heart above his head popped into my mind and I wanted to throw up. "How do you breathe if they take it out?" I was no science whiz, but didn't the heart have to pump oxygen through the blood or something?

"They've got machines for everything, Stef," Alice said. There was no nervous lilt to her voice or anything. "They're going to pump blood mechanically for a while."

Thelma looked up from her magazine. "What if there's a power outage?"

"For Pete's sake, Thelma. What kind of question is that?" Doris snapped.

Alice sighed and raised her hand, as if signaling

for silence. "They have a nurse riding a stationary bike in the basement that's attached to a generator. Happy now?"

This was one of the funniest things I'd ever heard. I'd always looked up to Alice, but right then, my admiration for her was at world-record-setting levels. She found the humor in everything, and at the same time, she managed to handle every crisis with such dignity and grace. I was so thankful to know her and grateful to have her as my best friend.

"So you're having surgery tomorrow?" I croaked.

Alice looked over at her IV and began fiddling with it. "Actually, they decided to do it this afternoon."

"This afternoon!" Doris and Thelma exclaimed in unison, equally horrified.

"Can I talk to Steffie alone for a minute?" Alice asked them.

They both wiped their eyes and left the room quietly.

"They took that well," she said. "Don't you think?"

I smiled as I sat down next to her. "I wish you'd told me you were sick. I could've helped you."

"Oh, Stef, that's all you needed—someone else to take care of. Besides, there's nothing you could've done." She grinned and squeezed my hand. "Anyway, I wanted to talk with you about Keith. He was just here," she said.

"I know," I said softly. "I saw him."

"He's such a sweet young man," Alice added.

"Yeah," I said, and then I paused. "Did he come here just to see you?"

I didn't mean it to come out sounding like it did, which was, *Why in the world would Keith come here to see you, of all people?*

But Alice just laughed. "Thelma brought me to the hospital last night, and she phoned Keith and asked him to bring over some of my medications because she didn't want to leave me. He came right over and then he dropped in again this morning."

Her explanation wasn't really that helpful. I was more curious as to *why* he'd taken the trouble to come to the hospital to see my best friend. Naturally, I didn't have to explain any of that to Alice because, as usual, she could read my mind.

"Keith will always be special to me too," she said. "I loved his mother—bless her heart—and I used to babysit for him when he was a little boy. After she died, well, I spent a lot of time with him. Then when his father started dating again, Keith went through a really hard time. He needed someone to talk to."

"And you were that person?" I asked.

She nodded.

I had to admit that the news that she and Keith were old friends was a total shocker. What other surprises was she going to spring on me? That Keith and I were siblings, separated at birth? Then it dawned on me.

"Wait a minute. Did you ask Keith to give me swimming lessons?"

She started fake coughing and pressing her call button. "Wow, I think I need to see the nurse."

I let go of her hand and crossed my arms in front of my chest. "Knock it off, Alice. Tell me the truth."

She sighed deeply. "Yes, I did. But I was worried about you. And that near-drowning incident really scared the crap out of me."

Everything suddenly fell into place. After all, I had wondered how someone like me (a pear girl who toted a plunger around) had caught his eye.

"No, Steffie," Alice said firmly. "Stop right there."

I wandered over to the window and peered outside. Jones Island seemed so tiny from up here.

"I know what you're thinking. I might have suggested the swimming lessons, but I most definitely did not suggest anything else. I can't say I was surprised to find out that he had become so fond of you. I knew that once he got close to you, well, he'd love you as much as I do."

Love? Had she just said *love?*

"He did mention one terrible mistake he made," Alice said coyly.

My mind flashed back to last night when I'd gone all

looney on him for having an ex-girlfriend. I knew exactly what he was referring to. "Let me guess. Going on a date with me?"

Alice chuckled. "You really are dense sometimes."

"What?" This was really not a great time for Alice to be laughing at me.

"He said Mora was the mistake. If it wasn't for her, he would have found you sooner."

Unfortunately, this information made me feel even worse. On top of not noticing that Alice had been sick, I had also overreacted the previous night. I was just so certain that my relationship with Keith would turn out the same way my mother's always did: with me being left alone and devastated when he returned to his girlfriend.

But before I could share any of this with Alice, we were interrupted by the nurse, who added another bag of clear liquid to Alice's IV. "We're going to start prepping you for surgery," she said to Alice. "I'm afraid your guest is going to have to leave."

My heart plummeted into the pit of my stomach as my breath caught in the middle of my windpipe. Alice and I looked at each other, both aware that it would've been a great time to make a joke, if we could have thought of anything to say.

Finally, Alice motioned toward her bedside table. "There's something in there I want you to have."

I opened the drawer. On top of a King James Bible, there was the notebook and pen that Alice used for her lists.

"I'm certainly not going to be needing them for a while," she said with a weak smile.

Despite her bravado, I could see the fear in her eyes. I was afraid too, but when I sat on her bed and hugged her tightly, I reminded myself that I had to be as strong for her as she'd been for me.

"You're my best friend, Alice," I whispered.

"And you're mine," she replied.

Doris, Thelma, and I went into the waiting room and planted ourselves on a pleather couch. There was no way any of us was going home until Alice was out of surgery. I couldn't speak for Doris and Thelma, but I didn't care how long it took. I was just going to camp out there in my maid outfit all night—all week, if need be.

I sat sandwiched between Doris and Thelma for what seemed like hours, watching lame soap operas and listening to Thelma and Doris argue. Every now and then I left them to duke it out while I perused the vending machine. Finally, the doctor came out to talk to us. The moment we saw him, we all held hands and braced ourselves for what turned out to be the best news I had ever received in my entire life.

Alice's surgery had gone so well that she would be

able to return home in a few days. After the doctor gave us her prognosis, he said with a knowing wink, "She's in great shape for a fifty-nine-year-old!" And of course, we all thought that was hilarious. Alice had been telling everyone that she was fifty-nine years old, but forgot that she was in a place with medical records and accurate dates of birth.

I left the hospital feeling as though Alice's illness had given me a new perspective on life. Her brief brush with the grim reaper, combined with Keith's confession about his dead mother, had made me feel grateful that I at least had a mom. I was determined to go home and turn over a new leaf. As I walked up the steps to my apartment building, I made a silent promise to the powers that be that no matter what, I would do my best to get along with Barbie from here on out.

Of course, that was before I knew she had progressed to stage seven: the finger move.

17

When I walked in the door, the map was spread out on the coffee table with a purple Sharpie beside it.

I heard a noise and turned. My mom was leaning against the kitchen doorframe. She looked terrible. Her mascara had run all over the place and her eyes were red and puffy. "How do you feel about Ellicott City?" she asked.

"You and the jackass broke up?" It was a dumb question to ask, because I already knew the answer.

"Oh, Stef," she said. And then came the waterworks.

The acid in my stomach started overflowing as the reality of what was happening began to sink in.

"If you could've heard him this morning, you just wouldn't have believed it," Barbie said. "I mean, how could this happen? Just yesterday, he told me he wanted to marry me. But now . . . now." She shook her head. "It's that daughter of his. Last night she tracked us down at the hotel where we were staying. She waited for us in the lobby and pounced just as we were about to go out to dinner. She told him she would never talk to him again if he left. She said she wanted nothing to do with him. She would never forgive him." Barbie looked at me, totally bewildered. "Can you believe that? And he bought it. Lock, stock, and barrel."

Honestly, I was impressed. He loved his daughter *so much* that he didn't want to hurt her. But apparently this concept was quite foreign to Barbie. "Well, she's his child," I said. "I'm sure he just wants to protect her."

"This isn't about her, Stef. He deserves some happiness in his life as well. I mean, she's not a baby, for God's sake. She's going to college in a couple years. Doesn't she want to see him happy?" Barbie's voice was shrill. "It's your whole generation. So selfish."

Selfish? What about her? Didn't she see herself as selfish? Her boyfriend was staying with a wife he didn't love because he didn't want to hurt his daughter. My mom, however, couldn't have cared less about me. She would've tossed me aside for him in a minute. She already had. This infuriated me.

"I don't want to move," I said sternly.

Barbie grabbed a tissue out of her zebra-print lounge-pants pocket and wiped her nose. "We don't have a choice, Stef. I can't stay here. I can't stand the thought of running into him with his happy little family."

I thought about how it would feel to leave everything behind again and start a new life in a new town with no Alice, no Keith, and no Tippecanoe. Although the maid job was crappy, I wouldn't have met either Alice or Keith if I hadn't worked there. Nothing could replace any of it.

"Keith is going back to school anyway," Barbie added. "And who knows what will happen when he gets back around all those college girls. . . ."

That was a low blow, and from the stunned look on Barbie's face, she knew it too.

I took a deep breath. "I can't do this anymore."

Barbie strode over to the couch, sat down, and began looking at the map. "What are you talking about?"

"I'm tired of dealing with your love lunacy," I said firmly. "I'm tired of your lies, I'm tired of moving, I'm tired of your hysteria and having to live my life with your crazy rules."

"Well, I am really, really sorry that you have it so bad," she said angrily. "I am so *sorry* to disappoint you."

The guilt trip wasn't working this time. I was going to stand my ground. "Oh, I am disappointed. In myself."

Barbie choked back some tears. "What do you mean?"

"I can't keep trying to save you, Mom." I stood motionless when I called her that, and so did she. At her request, I never called her Mom. She'd always wanted to be my pal instead of a mother figure. But that had never been what I needed. "If you want to move to Ellicott City, go ahead. But I'm not going anywhere."

She looked at me as her eyes filled with tears. "What are you going to do—move in with Alice or something?"

Actually, the idea had occurred to me.

My hesitation must have been obvious, because my mom took it as a big *Yes, I am moving in with Alice, you crazy lunatic!* and she snapped out of her sadness and responded every bit as maturely as I would've expected.

"Fine," she said irately. "Stay with Alice. Get your stuff and get out of here. As a matter of fact, I'll help you!"

Barbie stormed into the kitchen and grabbed a big black trash bag. She stormed into my room. "I'd hate to keep Alice waiting!" And then she yanked open my underwear drawer and dumped the contents into the bag. *"I'm going to be so happy living with an old lady."* She was imitating me by speaking in a really high, weird voice that made her sound like she had sucked in some helium. "Is that it, Stef? Or is it *I'm tired of watching you destroy your life!*"

I just shook my head, disgusted and disturbed by the whole performance.

"I need someone stable . . . ," my mother continued in her helium voice. "Well, living with Alice will be right up your alley, won't it? You guys can stay home all weekend and play bingo at the senior center and eat soft foods and talk about how much you hate me and what a crappy mother I am and how I'm a big fat failure at

every damn thing I do and how I've always treated you like crap and how no matter what I did or how much I tried it was never good enough for you . . ."

I turned away and walked slowly to the door as my mother continued to rant. For the second time in two days, someone left our apartment without saying goodbye.

It was nearly nine by the time I got to Keith's house. Fortunately, the whole scene with my mother had unnerved me so much that my entire body had gone numb. So numb that I wasn't even nervous about showing up uninvited. So numb that I rang the doorbell without hesitation, not even caring that Keith's parents might regard me as the girl who'd dashed their hopes of a Mora Cooper daughter-in-law and that they might therefore be not-so-happy to see me standing there in my maid uniform. But numb or not, I was still relieved when, after only a few seconds, Keith answered the door himself.

"Steffie? What's wrong?" he asked with concern. "Is it Alice?"

"She's fine," I replied. "The doctor thinks she might even come home in a few days."

"That's a relief." Keith was barefoot, wearing ripped jeans and a heather gray T-shirt that was fraying at the edges. His brown hair was all rumpled and tousled, and he had a little bit of stubble. He looked so cute that all my numbness faded away and I found myself fighting the urge to throw my arms around his neck and plant a big wet one on his lips.

"I appreciate you stopping by to tell me," he said. "I was worried about her."

"I figured," I said. "She told me that you guys were pretty close."

"Yeah," he said with a simple nod. "Alice is great."

I continued to stare at him, unable to look away. Why hadn't I just kept my mouth shut the previous night? How could I have let him leave?

"You must be tired," he said. "Have you been at the hospital all day?"

I nodded; then we shared an awkward pause.

"Well," he said finally. "Thanks again for letting me know how she was doing."

It was obvious that he was dismissing me. But I wasn't ready to leave, not yet at least. "I didn't," I announced before he could shut the door.

"Didn't what?"

"I didn't come here to tell you how Alice was doing. I came here because I wanted, I mean, *needed* to see you."

Wow, I was really going for broke. I'd never really admitted to "needing" anything in my life. But as I looked into Keith's eyes and thought about how brave

Alice had been in her darkest hour, I tried to muster enough courage to tell him how sorry I was and how I felt about him.

Keith hesitated a moment. I was hoping that he wasn't coming up with an excuse to send me away. "Um, do you want to come in? My dad and stepmother are at the beach house."

"Okay," I said in relief.

He led me through the marble-floored entranceway, past the white-on-white living room with the cathedral ceiling, and into a smaller (but definitely not small), dark, paneled room furnished with a black leather sectional, a big wood desk, and a giant flat-screen TV. The place was even more magnificent up close than it had appeared through Alice's binoculars.

"Do you want something to drink?" he asked politely.

"No thanks," I said breathlessly as I took in every inch of my surroundings.

I glanced at the bookshelves. They were lined with pictures of Keith from his glory days. Keith as captain of the Brucker's football team, making the touchdown that would win the game. Keith as a Cub Scout, making a leg splint out of some wood and an Ace bandage. There were more pictures as well, recent ones. Keith answering questions on some college quiz show . . . Keith reading *Moby-Dick* while lying in a hammock . . .

Keith giving a little girl a hug during a birthday party . . . and Keith and Mora dancing at the country club. I looked closely at that picture and studied the expression on Keith's face. He was frowning and his shoulders were slumped forward a bit, as if he couldn't wait for someone to cut in. This was when I realized that Keith and Mora were truly over, and all the irrational, envious feelings I had about their relationship suddenly vanished.

I turned to Keith and began my mea culpa. "I'm sorry for last night. I don't know what got into me. I had no right to talk to you like that."

He put his hands in his pockets and grinned a little. "It's okay."

"No, it's not okay." I sighed. "I shouldn't have panicked."

"You were feeling panicked?" Keith seemed very confused. "Why?"

I gazed into his kind brown eyes and was once again swept away by his charms. He was more than I'd ever hoped he'd be. A sweet, smart, sensitive (and gorgeous—like I'd forget that) guy who understood, just like me, what it was like to have a mother with serious issues.

"Well, because I was scared." I had to fess up to everything. Being honest with Keith was the only thing that would give us a real chance.

"Of what?"

I braced myself for the humiliation that might follow this admission. "I was afraid of getting love lunacy."

"Love lunacy," Keith repeated.

"Yes, it's what I call the sickness that makes my mom go all nuts whenever she falls for a married man."

Keith didn't flinch, so I kept explaining.

"So then I met you, and I liked you instantly, but you were with Mora and—"

"You thought you'd go nuts like your mom," he said, finishing my sentence.

"Right." I closed my eyes and waited for the snickering, but it never came. I opened my eyes and Keith was just standing there smiling widely.

"Stef, in a million years, you could never be like Barbie." He took a step closer to me. Six more and we'd be in lip-lock territory.

"Really?"

He sat down on the couch and motioned for me to join him. My whole body started to tingle as I sat next to him. He moved closer, putting his arm around me.

"Listen, if you were anything like her, I wouldn't want to spend every minute with you," he said. "The fact that you're Alice's friend speaks volumes. Stef, you're the most interesting person I've ever met."

This was the best thing I'd heard in my entire life. I touched his cheek as if trying to commit every second and every feeling to memory. I should've been on top of the world. After all, Keith still liked me. How great was that? Unfortunately, as happy and grateful as I was to get another opportunity to be with Keith, I still felt terrible.

"Are you panicking again?" he asked softly.

"It's not you. It's my mom." *Barbie*, I thought sadly. *It always came back to Barbie*. "That guy she was dating . . ."

"The married man?"

I nodded. "He broke up with her. So as per the final stage of love lunacy, she wants to move."

"When?"

"Tomorrow," I said. Keith placed a kiss on my cheek and I practically melted. "I don't want to go. I mean, I haven't talked to Alice, but I'm sure she'll let me stay there if I want."

Keith glanced away before gazing sadly into my eyes. "Look, Stef. I would love it if you stayed. Just knowing that I could see you for what's left of the summer and when I came back for vacations and stuff, well, it would make things so much easier. And believe me, I can relate to what you're going through. I know what it's like to have problems with your mom and want to get away from her for a while. But I think you should know that as troubled as my mother was, I'd give anything to see her again."

I shuddered once Keith was done talking. He was one hundred percent right. As much as I hated to admit it, I still loved my mother more than anything, and my place was with her, at least for now.

"I just don't want to say goodbye," I said, curling up in his arms, almost like a child.

Then Keith kissed me, and for once, I didn't think about my mother or love lunacy or Alice or what I would be doing tomorrow or the day after that. All I thought about was Keith and how lucky I was to be with him.

18

When I got home, around three in the morning, my mom was sitting on the couch, waiting for me. In all our years together, I had never seen her in such a bad state. She looked like she had just stuck a wet finger in an electrical outlet. Her hair was frizzy, her eyes were bloodshot, and her face was red and puffy. The apartment was a wreck as well. It looked completely ransacked. Various drawers, opened and empty, were scattered among full Hefty bags.

Barbie flipped her phone shut as her eyes filled with tears. "I was worried about you," she said. "I called everyone I could think of. I was just about to call the police."

"I'm sorry," I said sympathetically. "I went to see Keith."

"I called him too, but he didn't pick up."

"We didn't even hear the phone ring."

She glanced away. "I guess I had that coming, huh?"

"I honestly didn't hear it ring." I peered longingly at my bedroom door. I was exhausted. My day had been more frightening and thrilling than a marathon ride on Space Mountain.

"Why didn't you tell me about Alice?" she hiccupped.

I ran my fingers through my hair, which at that point had become a grease-fest from all the stress. "I didn't get a chance."

She stood up and took a step toward me. "I'm so sorry, Steffie."

I instinctively stepped backward. I wasn't in the mood for a makeup hug. "She's going to be okay."

"I know," she said. "I spoke to Thelma. I called over there, looking for you."

"Do you know where my pajamas are?" I nodded toward the mound of garbage bags outside my room. Barbie peeked inside one bag and then another.

She pulled out my nightshirt and handed it to me. "Here you go," she said cheerfully.

I took the nightshirt and headed to my room. Before I shut the door, I was overcome by an almost morbid sentimentality. I glanced back toward my mother and around the room where we had shared breakfasts and dinners and watched more hours of TV than I could count. "What time are we leaving tomorrow?" I asked quietly.

My mother's eyes grew wide as the meaning behind

my question sank in: I would be moving to Ellicott City with her.

"I'd like to leave as soon as possible." Her lower lip was quivering as she practically beamed motherly love. (In retrospect, it would've been a great time to ask her to buy me another pair of Michael Kors flip-flops.)

"Is it all right if we leave in the afternoon?" I asked. "I'd like to say a few goodbyes first."

"Sure." She choked back tears and smiled at me. "The afternoon would be fine."

I went to the hospital the next day. When I arrived at Alice's room with a bouquet of lilies in hand, I saw that her bed was empty. I had one moment where my heart stopped and I thought, *Oh-my-God-she-croaked*, before Doris and Thelma showed up and informed me that Alice had gone down for some tests and would be back in another hour or so. I guess I could've waited, but the truth of the matter was, I really couldn't bear the thought of saying goodbye to my best friend in all of North America. So I left Alice's notebook on top of her bed, along with a list I had made:

Reasons why you, Alice Anne Werner, will always be my best friend:

1) You know all the lyrics to "I Got You Babe" by Sonny and Cher.

2) You once told me *"mi casa es su casa."*

3) You can apply eyeliner, lipstick, and nail polish while driving eighty miles an hour down Route 50.

4) Every time you go grocery shopping, you always buy a half gallon of my favorite strawberry ice cream even though I know you can't stand it. (Because, as you've said numerous times, fruit has no business being in dessert.)

5) You're the only person who could make a job cleaning toilets fun.

6) When we went to Thelma's and she served pumpkin bread for dessert, you and I went back to your house and spent one hour analyzing why we've always hated pumpkin bread and another hour discussing who in their right mind would even consider pumpkin bread a dessert and another hour discussing whether a pumpkin is a fruit or vegetable.

7) You can make a list about anything.

8) You knew I would hate the movie *Gone with the Wind* before I even watched it. (And boy, were you right.)

9) You can always tell when I'm in a fake happy mood and you know exactly what to say to put me in an honest-to-goodness good one.

10) You asked Keith to teach me how to swim.

* * *

After the hospital, I went by Tippecanoe to quit my job. I said farewell to all the staff and then strolled down to the pool. When I walked through the gates, I kind of expected things to be different. Considering my new relationship with Keith and everything that had happened with Mora (not to mention the fact that I was no longer a maid), the whole social structure might have changed.

But it was exactly the same. Rafaela Berkenstein and her smarty-pants friends were off to the side, still discussing Sylvia Plath. Amy Fitz and her jocky friends were still doing cannonballs off the high dive, and Mora Cooper and the rest of the popular crowd were still talking on their gem-studded cell phones. The only difference was that there was a recent addition to the Mora group. One of the assistant golf pros, a hunky preppy-looking twenty-three-year-old, was sitting on Mora's lounge chair. Mora was giggling and rubbing some sunscreen on his shoulders. She seemed to sense my presence and looked my way. I held my breath, expecting some sort of confrontation. But nothing happened. In fact, her eyes barely registered me. She simply went back to rubbing sunscreen on the golf pro, laughing as he craned his head back and kissed her.

Keith was nowhere in sight, so I knocked on the door to the lifeguard office. Goatee Boy looked up from his clipboard. "Yeah?"

"Is Keith around?" I asked.

"No. He left this morning to go to his parents' beach house."

"This morning?" I had to do everything in my power not to faint.

"Yeah, his dad called him a little while ago. I guess he forgot something and asked Keith to bring it by."

The news that Keith had left hit me a lot harder than I would have expected. I hadn't planned on a big, gooey love scene, but I was hoping for some sort of exchange where we said how much we'd miss each other and what was on the horizon for us. Everything seemed so unfinished.

I rode my bike back home, crying like a toddler and moving as if in slow motion. My body seemed heavier, weightier, nearly impossible to manage. And my insides felt as if they were being crushed by a trash compactor. I was minutes away from hacking up my breakfast, so when I opened the door to my apartment, I had intended to make a mad dash to the bathroom. But I was blindsided by what I saw.

I was certain I was dreaming. It was as if the previous evening had never happened. The Hefty bags were gone, and the apartment looked exactly like it had two days before, with everything in its rightful place.

"I'm glad you're home," my mom said.

19

As soon as I'd finished hyperventilating, I made a mental note to add this to the Steffie Rogers's most-shocking-moments list.

"I don't understand," I said, trying to shake myself out of my stupor.

Barbie walked out of the kitchen, wiping her hands on her low-rise jeans. "You've made a lot of sacrifices for me, Stef. I decided that I wanted to make one for you."

I could barely contain my joy. "So we're staying?" I asked excitedly.

Barbie grinned. "Well, you really seem to like it here."

We are staying on Jones Island.

The realization that I would not have to leave Alice, that I would not have to move again and start my senior year at a new school, that I would be here when Keith returned on breaks and vacations, was enough to make me want to bend over and kiss the nasty orange carpet I was standing on. "Thank you," I said, throwing my arms around Barbie as if it was the most natural thing to do.

She held me tighter than she ever had. "I love you, Stef."

"I love you too," I said. In fact, I more than just loved her. I was glad she was my mother.

When Barbie and I were finished embracing, she said, "Thelma called to say that Alice really wants to see you before we leave. I told them we weren't moving after all and that we'd be over to see her this afternoon."

"That sounds great," I said merrily. "But there's one thing I want to do first. Do you know where my bathing suit is?"

Barbie's elation looked as though it was about to fade. "It's in your top drawer. Why?"

I thought about Alice in that instant and I knew she'd remind me not to lie to my mother, no matter how crazily she might react. So I didn't. "Because I thought I'd go for a swim."

She closed her eyes for a moment and I braced myself for the eruption. She breathed in deeply and then opened her eyes. "Have a . . . g-good time," she stammered.

And then (as if the hug wasn't enough), she kissed me on the cheek.

A half hour later, I was standing on the sand at Crab Beach and staring at the horizon. It was a warm, sunny day, and the calm water looked like an emerald green mirror. I swallowed my nervousness and began to walk toward it. I kept going without hesitation, wading in until the lukewarm water was up to my waist. I stopped for a moment, allowing my fingers to trail across the smooth surface as I practiced the stroke that Keith had taught me.

I kept telling myself over and over again, *You can do this.*

Then I took baby steps until the water was up to my chin. I cleared my mind, took a deep breath, and plunged forward. Salt water splashed up my nose as I wiggled around, moving my arms and kicking my legs. It was awkward at first, but the movements became smoother as my confidence increased and my rhythm steadied. But the truth of the matter was, I didn't care about my technique or how I looked. What mattered was that I had not sunk to the bottom of the bay. I was propelling myself through the water.

I felt as if I had achieved the impossible. I flopped around, twisting and splashing as I celebrated my independence. It was as if I had taken on the dark side and had not only survived, but conquered it as well. I was not my mother. I could swim.

After only a few minutes, I was both exhausted and

elated. I turned on my back and floated, allowing the tide to slowly pull me back to land. When my butt hit the sandbar, I stood up and turned toward shore. And that's when I saw Keith. He was sitting on the beach, watching my every move.

My heart fluttered as he grinned and stood up and began walking toward me. It amazed me that after fifty-eight days, he was still the most breathtaking thing I'd ever seen.

"I thought something came up at the beach house." I was shivering from the breeze so much that my teeth were chattering.

Keith smiled. "Well, I was driving up there when Alice called me and told me the good news. So I got ahold of my dad and told him he'd have to live without his wallet for a while." He stopped right in front of me and put his warm hands on my waist. "I saw you out there," he said softly. He didn't need to say anything else. I could practically see the pride in his eyes. I knew he understood just how much my solo venture into the water had meant to me.

He reached out and brushed the hair out of my eyes.

I knew without a doubt it was something a boyfriend would have done.

EPILOGUE

Steffie Rogers's all-time classic moments (in chronological order):

1) When the doctor said Alice was going to be all right.
2) When I found out that my mom had changed her mind about moving.
3) When I went swimming by myself (for the first time).
4) When I told my mom that I wanted to throw a party for Alice and she said (and I quote), "Sounds like fun."
5) When I got bit in the butt by a jellyfish and Keith had to put baking soda on my wound.
6) When Keith and I watched four hours of Animal Planet on his big-screen TV while sharing a

quart of strawberry ice cream (and eating right out of the container).

7) When Keith and I ran into Mora and her new golf-pro boyfriend at the grocery store and we all made two minutes (it seemed like twenty) of polite conversation before going our separate ways.

8) When I went over to Alice's house and we made a list (all the men she would like to kiss) while sitting in her white plastic chairs with our feet in the baby pool.

9) When my mom and I went to get mother-daughter matching manicures (I figured I owed her) and I let her choose the color (red) and the pattern (starbursts).

10) When (the night before he left for school) Keith told me he thought he had fallen in love with me.

Overall, the next two weeks were really busy and happy. In fact, ever since I'd found out that Alice was going to be okay, life had been so good that I sometimes had to pinch myself (not too hard) just to make sure I wasn't having some crazy wonderful dream. A lot of my good fortune was due to my mom, who was on her ultra-best behavior even though she was feeling lousy. Normally, two weeks after a breakup, Barbie was pretty much back to normal, and I wasn't sure whether she had just really liked this guy more than the others or it was more difficult this time because she couldn't run away, but she hadn't stopped crying.

But at the risk of sounding like Suzy Sunshine, I hadn't given up hope that maybe, just maybe, her decision to stay on Jones Island would force her to deal with her love lunacy once and for all. She'd never really had to deal with the repercussions of her disease before (like that Sunday when we ran into "the jackass" and his wife at the Red Lobster and he totally ignored us). Some unpleasant run-ins with the jackass might encourage her to think twice the next time a married man came on to her. (I said *might*.)

But even if she didn't think twice, I had come to the realization that there was nothing I could do about it (honest). And, although I couldn't promise her that I'd turn the other cheek and ignore it, I did promise to at least *attempt* to keep my sentiments to myself. It would be a lot easier to do, considering that I had my own love life to think about. Which (according to Alice) had become the talk of the island. Everyone (according to Thelma) had been wondering if Keith and I had done it before he left for school. (I was sorry to disappoint everyone, but the answer was a big no.)

I had the feeling that Barbie, however, didn't really believe me. She probably thought I had gone all the way and just didn't want to tell her. And weirdly enough, she seemed to like that. I guess it made me seem a little bad. Which to Barbie was good.

I realized that not scoring a home run made me a candidate for virginal geekdom (at least a temporary one), but I had had enough excitement lately, thank you very much. How much trauma/drama could a girl take? Besides, every time I thought about giving it up, I heard my mom's voice in my head, describing how beautiful her first time was and how she would remember it for the rest of her life. And that alone was enough to make me think twice.

As far as I was concerned, I figured it might be nice to save something for later. . . .